Speaking of bodies, Lauren was evidently enjoying a very nice eyeful of Sebastian's

This time, he realized, she wasn't searching for something neutral to focus on when she spoke to him. "You know, there's something I should do before I forget." She scooted next to him and placed a hand on his thigh.

"You need to check that police source for your story?" He observed her hand.

"Yeah, I need to do that, but that wasn't what I had in mind at the moment." She made a slow circle on his skin with her index finger.

"You need to call room service for something to eat? I realize we missed dinner." Sometimes his gallantry astounded him.

"No, I'm fine."

Sebastian tweaked a smile. "You're absolutely right, darlin'—in fact, you're a lot more than fine," he whispered as Lauren undid her terry-cloth robe and let it slip from her shoulders.

Dear Reader,

The life of a reporter is often filled with uninspiring daily assignments. But what if, under unusual circumstances, a reporter actually got to exercise a self-indulgent flight of fancy regarding one of the least-coveted of duties—writing an obituary?

What if, indeed?

Lauren Jeffries finds out the repercussions when an obituary that she has liberally embellished inadvertently gets published. Not only is her journalistic integrity compromised, but she also finds herself enmeshed in an international art theft. And even more dangerously, she tangles with Sebastian Alberti, the investigator on the case.

Never has a case of "misapplied" identity led to so many twists and turns and sexy interludes. Yes, those sexy interludes.

And here I said a reporter's life was dull!

All the best,

Tracy Kelleher

Books by Tracy Kelleher

HARLEQUIN TEMPTATION
908—EVERYBODY'S HERO
949—IT'S ALL ABOUT EVE...

TRACY KELLEHER

THE TRUTH ABOUT HARRY

HARLEQUIN®

TORONTO • NEW YORK • LONDON
AMSTERDAM • PARIS • SYDNEY • HAMBURG
STOCKHOLM • ATHENS • TOKYO • MILAN • MADRID
PRAGUE • WARSAW • BUDAPEST • AUCKLAND

To my gracious editor, Kathryn Lye.
You made it happen.

ISBN 0-373-69194-7

THE TRUTH ABOUT HARRY

www.eHarlequin.com

Printed in U.S.A.

Prologue

Harry Nord, 83, Manufacturer And Philanthropist, Dies

Harry Nord, a decorated World War II pilot, self-made millionaire and generous local philanthropist, died in his sleep yesterday at the Philadelphia Veteran's Administration Hospital. He was 83 years old and had been ill for some time.

A true Horatio Alger story, Mr. Nord, born in Camden, New Jersey, came from a humble background, having been orphaned at the age of twelve when his parents died in the infamous B&O train crash of December 1934. An investigation of the incident revealed that the conductor had reported to work inebriated after celebrating at the company Christmas party. Charges were leveled, though later dropped, against the railroad's management. Mr. Nord liked to tell employees of Nord Notions and Trimmings Company, of which he was founder and president, that it was his constant lack of proper winter clothing growing up in greater Philadelphia that led him to the garment industry.

Before making his mark in the industry, Mr.

Nord had a distinguished military career in World War II, rising to the rank of captain. A pilot, his plane was shot down on a mission over northern Italy. Although dazed and injured, Mr. Nord dragged his wounded navigator from the burning plane. Local villagers of San—

LAUREN JEFFRIES tapped on the space bar and rubbed her lips. "San what?" she asked out loud to no one in particular. The rest of the Metro Desk at the *Philadelphia Sentinel,* eastern Pennsylvania's second-largest newspaper—a claim that never failed to generate a snide "Hah!" from Lauren—had long since filed their stories for the night's deadline and were drinking cheap beer and complaining about their piddly salaries at Gino's, the bar around the corner from the office.

She glanced at her notes, knowing already that they wouldn't offer any assistance. A conspiratorial smile formed on her lips, and she hunched over her terminal and tapped furiously.

Local villagers from San Margherita discovered the two men and hid the crew until they were well enough to travel. Then, with the aid of a shepherd, they hiked to safety across the Alps to Switzerland. Mr. Nord was later awarded a Bronze Star for heroism.

Upon conclusion of the war, Mr. Nord returned to Philadelphia, where he secured various entry-level jobs in the garment industry. While working as a buttonholer at a shirt factory, he realized that the finishing process would proceed much more quickly if there were a single machine that could sew and slit the buttonholes at the same time. He developed an automatic buttonhole device, which he patented. The Nordomatic, as the device came to be known, revolutionized shirtmaking. Later inventions, including the zigzag zipper-foot, further established Mr. Nord as an innovative leader in the industry, and laid the groundwork for Nord Notions and Trimming Company, a manufacturing business whose headquarters were once located next to Thirtieth Street Station. In 1991, the Singer Corporation bought out Nord Notions; operations were subsequently moved to Mexico.

Mr. Nord was a generous benefactor, as well as an industrial leader. Locally, he established the "Winter Coat Drive" to aid the Salvation Army. Perhaps his most generous act of charity—

Lauren backspaced and deleted the last word.

—of largesse was the rebuilding of the tiny town of San Margherita. Grateful for the protection the villagers had offered despite the risk to their own safety, Mr. Nord donated funds to build a new school, retirement home and library, restore the community's small but noteworthy Romanesque church and establish a scholarship program to send promising students to universities in Italy and abroad. A plaque in his honor, affixed to the north wall of the town hall, proclaims in Italian, "Here he came to earth in a blaze of fire, and with God's help, raised San Margherita from the ashes."

Lauren leaned back. The quote was outrageous, and she could just see Dan Jankowski, the copy editor on duty that night, chuckling to himself before he hit the delete button and sent her a terse e-mail: "Try to keep your flights of fancy to under three inches. This is Metro, not Page One."

It was bad to fabricate the story, even an obit. Really bad. Lauren, who wore professional integrity on her sleeve the way a lot of professional athletes had endorsement patches, knew it more than most. But she couldn't help it. And it wasn't like this one was ever going to see the light of day. Call it a revenge piece. A catharsis. A way to vent her reporter's spleen. She'd just found out that her managing editor, Ray Kirkel, the douche bag, had passed her over for the State House reporter job in favor of Huey Neumeyer. Huey! An editorial assistant who couldn't even photocopy straight. Maybe the fact that he was Ray's wife's cousin had something to do with the appointment.

"Everything to do with it!" Lauren snorted. One did not grow up in South Philly without acquiring a certain sense of cynicism. It was like cheesesteaks, the local culinary specialty—it went with the territory.

After three years pounding the Metro beat, generating more than the usual school board and two-alarm fire stories—and garnering an award from the Pennsylvania Press Association for her piece on teenage runaways—what did she get? A fax tossed on her desk and an order from Ray: "Two inches by deadline. An ad was pulled from the obit page, and I need to fill the space."

Lauren had looked down at the bare-bones release from the mortuary. Harry Nord, the real Harry Nord, wouldn't guarantee more than half a column inch, and that was with a free plug for the funeral parlor.

"So, this is my reward for all my hard work and effort?" Lauren wailed silently after Ray had waddled off in the direction of the men's room. "The man wouldn't know a crack reporter, let alone a crack story, if he fell over one," she muttered under her breath. And to prove her point, she'd taken Harry Nord's death notice and embellished it beyond recognition, turning it into the human interest story of the year, knowing full well it wouldn't run, but getting a genuine sense of satisfaction nonetheless.

Tomorrow, she'd do the real obit on the real Harry Nord, and it would appear in a late edition. Ray would never know. As far as she could tell, he hardly ever looked at the paper except to scan the six-column photos of buxom, bikini-clad babes.

Without a second thought, Lauren hit Send and forwarded the text to the Copy Desk. End of story.

Yeah, right.

1

"I AM SO SCREWED," Lauren mumbled into the shoulder of her fuzzy sweater. She slowly rubbed her forehead as if willing her headache to escape via the horizontal tracks she was tunneling in her cranium.

"What's that?" Phoebe Russell-Warren arched her swanlike neck and thrust her shoulders back to get a better view of the television news conference at the front of the office lobby. At six foot one with impeccable posture—the effects of years of field hockey, she had once assured Lauren—Phoebe cut an impressive figure. The major bits of gold hanging off her earlobes and dangling from her slender wrists added to the Amazonian effect. "You don't recognize the man standing next to Ray, do you?" she asked, peering elegantly ahead. "I know all the local broadcasters, at least those worth knowing, and he doesn't look familiar."

Phoebe wasn't exaggerating her people skills. As Lifestyle editor, she knew everyone on Society Hill *and* the Main Line with a trust fund and a Porsche Boxster.

Lauren went up on tiptoe and frowned. "I can't see anything clearly except Baby Huey's dandruff on his navy blue blazer." Unlike Phoebe, Lauren barely grazed the five-foot-three mark, even wearing clogs. Clogs, a turtleneck sweater and khaki pants—ah, yes, the wardrobe of the penurious and fashion-challenged reporter.

Phoebe turned her attention away from the news conference and stared down at Lauren. "What was it you said? Baby Huey?"

"It's my new name for Neumeyer, intrepid State House reporter and genuine turd," Lauren said, gripping her take-out coffee cup a little harder than necessary.

"Ladies and gentlemen," Ray Kirkel, their fearless leader, intoned by the bank of glass doors, "I'm very excited to welcome you all here today for this important announcement."

There was a pause. Lauren figured Ray was beaming into the television cameras from the local affiliate of the network news.

"Not that we're not used to excitement on a regular basis here at the *Sentinel*," he started up again.

"I wish you could see the man at the front next to Ray. He is an absolute dish." Phoebe nudged Lauren.

Only Phoebe could get away with phrases like "an absolute dish," Lauren thought. Lauren breathed in slowly and reluctantly leaned toward her friend. "Forget Dishy Mystery Man for a moment."

"Forget him? Are you crazy? He has that dangerous look of a young Sean Connery playing James Bond. Maybe he has a Scottish accent, too? Nothing like a Scottish accent in bed. Or in the shower. Or up against the wall."

Lauren went back to rubbing her forehead.

"Phoebe, listen, I have something important that I really need to tell you." The need to bare her soul was an unfortunate attribute of Lauren's, and one that at the age of twenty-seven she hoped she would have left behind—the same way she'd cleared up her teenage acne and shed the fifteen pounds of puppy fat that once surrounded her waist like a plastic float.

"We're gathered here today because of the passing of a great man," Ray bellowed.

Phoebe reluctantly shifted her gaze to Lauren. "You need to confess something? The woman who doesn't sleep around, indulge in illegal substances and only drinks wine or beer—and then in moderation? You won't even buy me cigarettes when I run out."

Lauren rolled her eyes. "It's about the obit," she whispered.

"The obit?" Phoebe's delivery wasn't quite so sotto voce.

"Shh!" Baby Huey turned around. "You two are interrupting a unique moment here." He looked at them sternly before shifting back to take in the action.

"If you only knew how unique," Lauren moaned softly.

"As usual, the *Sentinel* came through," Ray continued before raising his arm magisterially and pointing to a screen that had been set up to his right. Instantly, there appeared a giant image—an obituary. Lauren's obit. Well, not her actual obit, but the obit she'd written.

"It just shows that with the right editorial guidance, even a junior member of the staff can make an impact," Ray announced.

Lauren groaned. "Maybe he won't mention my name."

"Of course he won't mention your name. Ray is a total asshole," Phoebe said sympathetically.

"Once more, I'm pleased to say our paper, despite our limited resources in comparison to television, scooped the other media." Ray modestly held up his hand. "No slight to you folks," he joked to the TV crews. *Yeah, right.*

"Maybe now I'll find out who Mr. Tall, Dark And Handsome is." Phoebe didn't bother to be coy as she started to move forward through the crowd.

Lauren reached out and stopped her. "Phoebe, there's something you need to know about the obit." She gulped. "The guy's story— I made the whole thing up." She'd like to say she felt better for confessing, but the pit in her stomach was only getting larger.

"Wha-at?" Phoebe squawked. She swiveled around and grabbed Lauren by both forearms.

"Those Pilates classes have really improved your grip," Lauren observed.

"Actually, it's high-impact yoga." Phoebe pulled her closer and bent her head down. "You mean you killed off somebody who wasn't dead."

Lauren shook her head. "No, trust me, Harry Nord is good and dead." She cast a worried glance around to see if anyone was watching.

Who was she kidding? With two women locked in an embrace, of course somebody was watching. "Will you keep it down? All the guys in production will think we're staging a little snuggle here just for their benefit." Lauren grabbed Phoebe by the shoulders, hustled her down the hallway and pushed her through the first door they came to.

Phoebe looked around. "If you're worried what people are going to think, squirreling me away into the janitor's closet is not going to help." Unfazed, she overturned a large mop bucket and lowered herself regally, crossing one leg over the other so that her taupe patent leather Chanel pump swung gracefully next to her slender calf.

Lauren scraped her loose bangs from her forehead. "You see, it's like this. Ray, being the asshole he is—as you so rightly pointed out—not only appointed Baby Huey to the State House reporter's job over me, but he didn't even have the nerve to tell me to my face. I heard it from Donna."

"You mean, Donna of the ill-fitting double-Ds? She won't ever give me new erasers, even when I ask politely." In addition to being president of the Engelbert Humperdinck Fan Club, Donna Drinkwater was head of the supply closet and ruled over it with the arbitrary élan of a born martinet.

"You're kidding? I can always get erasers," Lauren said, then waved her hand in the air. "The point is, Ray, the schmuck, when he finally did come face-to-face, merely assigned me an obit without so much as a by-your-leave. So I got mad, really mad. And really more out of spite than anything, I—"

Phoebe rose. "You don't need to go on. You invented a great news story—about Harry Nord—didn't you?"

Lauren nodded.

"You know, I particularly liked the bit about the villagers harboring Harry and his wounded navigator after he dragged him from their burning plane."

"Thanks a lot. Anyhow, never in my wildest dreams did I expect the thing to appear."

"Of course not." Phoebe laughed, then did a double take. "Are you telling me you submitted it to the Copy Desk and counted on them to realize it was a joke?"

"To my utter amazement, all Dan Jankowski did was change a semicolon to a period. Did you ever notice the way Dan hates semicolons?"

Phoebe eyed her gravely.

Lauren held up her hand. "I know, I know. It was a stupid thing to do. But how was I to know that the story would run, that it would get picked up by the wire services and somehow find its way to television?" She breathed in deeply. "Do you think I should throw myself on Ray's mercy and hope that in his heart of hearts he'll find a way to forgive me?"

"Lauren, get real. Ray doesn't have a heart." Phoebe paused. "Have you ever thought about becoming a salesperson in the shoe department at Wanamaker's?" As an old-time Philadelphian, Phoebe still referred to the department store in the grand building on Market by its original name— steadfastly refusing to let Lord & Taylor pass her lips. "I could really use the discount."

"Phoebe! This is my career we're talking about."

Actually, it was more like her life's dream—not the part about working for the *Sentinel* necessarily, but being a reporter. Ever since Lauren could remember, she had been hooked on journalism. She salivated over the way the headlines screamed the news. Marveled at the quotes that the writers could get important people to say. Was awestruck by the emotions the photos could elicit. Even the smell of the newsprint and the way the ink came off on her fingers inspired Lauren with a sensory glee that she couldn't explain—certainly not to her mother, who naturally thought Lauren should join the family dry cleaning business and certainly not break off her engagement to a handsome local boy who had a guaranteed income of seventy thousand as an accounts manager at Jefferson Memorial Hospital.

"Just think, he could probably use his influence to get you a private room at a lower rate when you have your first baby," her mother liked to say. This from the woman who saved used rubber bands on the kitchen doorknob.

Well, despite her mother's protests, Lauren *had* pulled the plug on the whole rosy picture—the baby, the private hospital room and the wedding.

The decision had been made easy when she found her fiancé, the no-good creep Johnny Budworth, doing the deed with Agnes Iolites, their greatly overpriced wedding planner. But that wasn't the only thing that had tipped the scales. You see, Lauren had already wised up to the fact that Johnny never understood what turned her on— and she wasn't just talking about sex, though sex was part of it. Over the course of their relationship, Lauren had seriously wondered if halftime during a televised Eagles game really *was* the most romantic moment to indulge in intercourse.

No, it was more than about sex. And if she had

to put her finger on the one thing that summed up their different outlooks on life it would be that Johnny never read her articles, never read the *Sentinel*—never read *any* newspaper for that matter. "I listen to news radio, babe. What more do I need to know?" he'd say, and then add, "You know, maybe you should go wash your hands. The ink from the paper leaves smudges on the white leather couch my Aunt Dotty gave me."

Yeah, it was more than a career for Lauren—it was a dream of doing something special, making a difference, regardless of leaving smudges. The *Sentinel* might not be the end-all-be-all, but it was on the road to better things.

Phoebe placed a hand on Lauren's shoulder. "Listen, if I were you, I'd just stay quiet. Who knows? There's a good chance that this whole thing will blow over and no one will ever know. Besides, it's not like the story ran with a byline, and Ray's not about to voluntarily give you any credit."

Lauren was tempted to tell Phoebe she'd split an infinitive, but decided now was probably not a good time. "Maybe you're right. Maybe it'll all blow over like yesterday's news." And maybe she'd grow another four inches.

Lauren squared her shoulders. "So, shall we go back and see the rest of the dog and pony show?"

Phoebe nodded, and they slipped out of the closet—so to speak.

"I am especially pleased that the *Sentinel* is able to have yet another scoop," Lauren heard Ray announce when they got back to the large lobby. "And with that in mind, it is my great pleasure that I am able to introduce to you today—"

Lauren went up on her tiptoes and strained to see the front of the room.

"Sebastian Alberti."

"Who?" Lauren looked to Phoebe who had abandoned her customary sangfroid and was violently fanning herself.

"The grandson of Philadelphia's own hero, Harry Nord," Ray declared.

Just as the Red Sea parted for Moses, so too the bodies in the lobby miraculously opened up, and for the first time Lauren got a good look. At Ray. No, forget Ray. At the man standing next to Ray.

She was stunned. No wonder Phoebe had gone gaga. Men like that simply didn't live in Philly. They didn't even visit Philly. They certainly didn't walk through the front door of the *Sentinel*'s lobby.

And nothing against Phoebe's judgment, but Sean Connery, even younger and *with* hair, couldn't hold a candle to the man in front. Tall, with broad shoulders and a trim build, Sebastian Alberti wore his charcoal-gray suit as if it were made for him. Lauren peered more closely—it was probably made for him. Still, even though he looked perfectly at home in Savile Row tailoring, he was definitely no wimpy clotheshorse. Not when his confident posture managed to simultaneously radiate ease and tension.

And that face. Lauren shook her head. *Face* was too prissy a word. His collection of chiseled features—the prominent cheekbones and square jaw—his raven-black hair, deep-set eyes and slashing eyebrows. No question about it, the whole package spelled B-A-D. Hot bad. Hot, HOT bad.

With some coaxing, Sebastian Alberti stepped to the microphone and smiled. At which point his features altered perceptibly, and a collective sigh could be heard from among the female members of the audience and even some of the guys, though not the boys from production. Right in front of their eyes, Mr. Bad Boy was transformed into Mr. Bad Boy With A Heart.

Lauren would have succumbed then and there along with all the others duly affected in the room. Would have—except for one glaring problem. Harry Nord, real or otherwise, didn't have a grandson.

Sebastian Alberti—or the heartthrob claiming to be Sebastian Alberti—leaned into the microphone and ducked his head down, just like someone not used to talking in front of an audience. Lauren could feel the tension as all the mothering types held themselves back from going up and adjusting the angle of the mike just so.

"I'm honored to be here today. Thank you, Ray." He nodded politely, and Ray lifted a hand and pretended to be humble. "I never thought anyone would write about my grandfather that way." Unlike Double-O-Seven and his Scottish burr, Harry's supposed grandson spoke in a subtle southern drawl. But it definitely contained a license to kill. Hearts, that is.

"My late mother, a product of war-torn Italy—" a chorus of "oohs" chimed in here "—would have been so pleased that her father was finally recognized, given his generosity to her small village. *Babbo*, as I always called him, never talked about his past. 'True giving,' he always said, 'should be anonymous.'"

There was a chorus of "amens."

"It's like watching a revivalist minister in an Armani suit," Lauren said out of the side of her mouth.

"Well, I could easily become a convert," Phoebe nearly panted.

"So, given how difficult it must have been to unearth this story—"

"Not that difficult," Lauren whispered.

"I find myself just wanting one thing—"

Lauren saw Donna Drinkwater instinctively step forward.

"And that's to meet the intrepid reporter who uncovered my *babbo*'s story." He lifted his chin and scanned the crowd. His eyes quickly honed in on the back corner of the room, the back corner where Lauren was crushing her foam cup and trying to look even smaller than she already was.

Phoebe coughed. "Tell you what. As long as we're making things up, how about I be you? For him, I'm ready and willing to be totally screwed."

2

"CAN YOU BELIEVE RAY didn't announce the guy's name until the very end? Talk about burying the lead!" Lauren complained into the mirror of the ladies' room. She had to lean to the right because the notice to buy Tupperware from Elaine in Accounting was taped smack in the middle of the glass.

"Forget Ray's journalistic failings." Phoebe rummaged through a small Fendi pouch containing makeup. "You're on the verge of possibly being fired. There are far bigger issues to worry about. Apricot or pink?"

Lauren looked at the two tubes in Phoebe's hand. "You criticize me for discussing journalistic competence when you're debating the merits of lip gloss?"

"This is not simply a matter of lip gloss. We're talking about your image as you're about to face Ray and Harry Nord's grandson."

"Phoebe, how many times do I have to tell you? Harry Nord never had a grandson."

"Are you sure?"

Lauren nodded. "According to the press release from the funeral parlor, the real Harry Nord had no family survivors."

"Well, the fake one—the one you invented—appears to have acquired one, and, trust me and my little heart, which is still going pitter-patter, *he* is very real."

Lauren tipped her head. "You're right."

Phoebe surveyed her with an arched brow. "And frankly, even though you are one of my nearest and dearest, you are hopeless in the image department. I mean, really, that ersatz-graduate-student look of chinos and clogs is so passé."

Lauren held her hands out wide and looked down at herself critically. Okay, not that critically. "And here I thought wearing an eggplant mock turtleneck sweater was daring. What did I know?"

"Obviously, not enough. Darling, extreme décolletage is daring." Phoebe thrust a tube toward her. "Here, take the pink. We'll simply play up your baby-fine blond hair—capitalize on that innocent look of yours."

Lauren stared at the lip gloss and did as she was told. Innocence was a rare commodity these days, as she knew only too well. She tossed her cold cup of coffee into the trash, turned to Phoebe and, holding herself erect, declared, "I can do this." She punched the air and pushed open the bathroom door—

And ran smack into trouble, aka Sebastian Alberti. To be more precise, the top of her head plowed into his pronounced and very hard chin. Which left her momentarily stunned. She put out a wobbling hand and connected with something hard, very hard. And it wasn't the door.

The material of his designer suit may have been soft as silk, but the fabric of the body underneath was as solid as marble, and as well-chiseled as a Rodin statue. Sebastian Alberti might be a phony, but there was nothing insubstantial about him.

Lauren attempted one of those cleansing breaths that relaxation gurus are so fond of. To say that inner calm was hard to achieve when her nose was pressed into a silk tie and her nostrils were filled with the heat and woodsy scent of a drop-dead gorgeous male was something of an understatement. Still, calm, or the illusion of calm, was absolutely essential if she had any hope of rescuing her career—and her sanity.

She pulled her head back and looked up, her eyes level with a half-Windsor knot. "Sorry, I didn't see you coming."

Sebastian Alberti rubbed his chin, then dropped his hand and smiled a heartbreaking, melt-in-your-mouth-and-on-the-gray-industrial-carpeted-floor smile. "That makes two of us."

Lauren nearly sank back into him with more than her nose. But propelled by an even stronger sense of professional decorum, she mustered what little self-control she still had and took a step back. "Yes, well, um…" Words were supposed to be her forte. "You might not realize this, but we're actually supposed to see each other in Ray's office." She gulped. "I'm Lauren Jeffries, the reporter who wrote *your grandfather's* obituary." The dramatic emphasis could have registered as far south as Baton Rouge.

Her words seemed to ruffle—albeit momentarily—his composure. Was it a flash of surprise or sexual interest?

Foolishly, Lauren was hoping that sexual interest would win out. She shook her head. Foolishly was right. She hadn't been foolish since she'd cooed over the engagement ring that Johnny Budworth had given her when he'd proposed at an Outback Steakhouse. She'd actually believed that the sparkling brilliant had been genuine and not cubic zirconia from the Home Shopping Network.

Fool me once, shame on you. Fool me twice, shame on me, as the saying went. Lauren looked up at the small cleft in Sebastian Alberti's chin—such a nice cleft, by the by—and said out loud the obvious. No, not that she found him amazingly attractive and would desperately like to throw caution to the wind and check into the Four Seasons and have wild, abandoned sex and use all the bath towels. But rather, "I think it's safe to assume we have much to discuss about our situation here."

He arched a brow. "You think?"

"I know and you know," she said emphatically, with a lot more confidence than she was feeling.

He crooked up the corner of his mouth. "Meaning that our involvement makes us both—"

"Liars?" she offered.

A sexy dimple appeared in his right cheek as his smile broadened. "And here I was going to say soul mates."

Lauren looked into Sebastian Alberti's dark eyes—up close they were a deep, sinfully dark, chocolate brown. If they were supposed to be the windows to his soul, then she was in real trouble.

She swallowed. And was saved from coming up with some witty, sophisticated reply by a loud rapping from the other side of the ladies' room door.

Phoebe maneuvered her head around the corner. "Is it safe to come out yet?"

"It all depends on what you mean by safe." Lauren waved her through. "Phoebe Russell-Warren, Sebastian Alberti. Phoebe is the *Sentinel*'s Lifestyle editor.

He nodded. "It's not every day I get to meet a Lifestyle editor." He was the very embodiment of charm, but was it Lauren's imagination, or had the tension that had zinged back and forth a second ago like a cue ball ricocheting off the side pocket, instantly lessened?

Not that that deterred Phoebe. "Well, it's not every day I get to meet the grandson of one of our obituaries." She smiled broadly, displaying the dazzling effect of diligent dental care.

Sebastian smiled smoothly. "And it's not every day that you get an obituary like my grandfather's, either, is it?"

"You're darn tootin'," Ray greeted them, his enlarged waist preceding the rest of him by a second or two. "Well, I see you've already met the little lady who wrote the story." He nodded to Lauren.

She closed her eyes and told herself she would not lecture Ray on his choice of words.

"I would hardly call Ms. Jeffries little in terms of her capabilities," Sebastian said.

That opened Lauren's eyes.

Phoebe's eyes were already locked on Sebastian's in killer seduction mode. "I bet your capabilities aren't little, either—in any terms."

Sebastian raised one eyebrow. "You know, I'm

beginning to wonder why I never met a Lifestyle editor before."

Lauren went back to rubbing her forehead.

"Maybe I can run a feature on you?" Phoebe offered, stepping close enough to discern the warp and woof of his suit jacket. *Woof* was right.

"Don't be ridiculous." Ray wagged a finger at Phoebe. "You've got a luncheon to go to or whatever it is you do."

"I only fill six pages on weekdays and a half section on Sunday, but then, don't mind me," Phoebe huffed before turning to Lauren. "Let me know if there's anything I can do to help." On the last word, she looked pointedly at Sebastian and inhaled loudly before sauntering off in regal fashion.

"Is she for real?" Sebastian asked as he watched Phoebe depart, her long legs striding and her narrow hips swaying around the corner.

"I sometimes wonder myself," Lauren admitted. "I think it has something to do with going to too many cotillions at an impressionable age."

"Ray—Ray, we've got a situation." Huey Neumeyer bounded over—definitely not a pretty sight in Lauren's opinion. Here was a man who wouldn't know a cotillion if he tripped over one. Actually, tripping was his usual mode of entrance.

"We've got reports of a hostage situation at the State House, but I'm here because of the press conference and not in Harrisburg to cover the story," Huey panted. A rivulet of perspiration meandered down his right cheek, and a distinct whiff of body odor mixed with Aramis.

Lauren smelled a story—among other things.

"I've got a source in the State House. And I have his cell phone number," she volunteered. The minority leader's chief of staff had been the best man at her brother's wedding, and during the rehearsal dinner they'd shared a few too many tequilas, along with several wet kisses and a quick feel. Since all the action had stayed above the waist, it meant he was still a reliable source.

Huey stamped his foot. "This is my beat."

Sebastian wisely sidestepped Huey's little hissy fit. "Not that I want to get in the way of a pressing news story, but I was ever so hoping to meet up with Ms. Jeffries." He turned his southern drawl up another notch.

"Huey, pull yourself together and go to my office," Ray barked, his face turning an alarming shade of red. Lauren wondered if she should send him an e-mail suggesting the merits of a stress test. "I'll get the governor's press secretary on the phone and the spokesperson for the Pennsylvania State Police. You can head out with a photographer as soon as we know what's happening. And you, Jeffries—" Ray jabbed an index finger in the air in front of her sweater "—take Mr. Alberti to the conference room. And don't even think about calling your source and muscling in on this story."

Forget the e-mail, Lauren thought as she watched him lumber down the hall. She spun around and was immediately aware that she was alone with Sebastian.

"I believe you were going to show me the conference room?" he asked.

A sense of foreboding overcame her. She nodded

toward the hallway. "This way." She didn't bother to linger and, instead, quickly clomped down the linoleum floor to the open door at the end. She sounded like a Clydesdale. Maybe clogs weren't the best shoe choice after all.

"Here we are, Mr. Alberti." She pushed the door open. "Is that your real name, by the way?" She waited for him to go through first.

Sebastian paused in the doorway and thought, *now's the time to bring out the truth, at least, carefully edited portions of the truth.* "Please, as a Southerner and an Italian, custom prevents me from preceding a lady through the door." He waited. "And my name really *is* Sebastian Alberti. Actually, Sebastiano Alberti, but I anglicized it years ago."

That was only one of the changes he'd made when he was young—not that change solved everything.

Sebastian had long ago learned to accept the notion that he was destined to be an outsider, no matter how much he adapted. He had left Italy as a child. The land of Valentino and Visconti had grown and altered, and so had he. There was no way it could ever be home again.

Nor could Alabama be, either. His family had moved to the deep South. Their strange accent was noticeable—their ignorance of the great god Bear Bryant even more egregious. Sebastian had arrived having never thrown a baseball and never eaten fried chicken. He immediately devoted himself to becoming the most American of Americans. Ah, the fervor of a convert.

But never mind that he played tight end in high

school and dated a cheerleader. He was still different, never fully accepted. His mother made sure of the latter—having run off with the rival high school's football coach when he just started junior high.

Still, he couldn't blame all of his sense of alienation on his mother. He had never completely fit in because, well, he just never had. No amount of time could erase the moments when he yearned to bite into crusty Italian bread instead of eating hush puppies, when he would have given anything for a bowl of creamy risotto instead of gravy on mashed potatoes.

But the anxiety of being an outsider that had so plagued him during his teenage years had gradually subsided. Now it was something he actually cultivated like a protective cloak, a cloak that even extended to his place of residence.

Besides his farm in the country, miles from anyone else, he had a small but tasteful townhouse in Georgetown. His neighbors were diplomats—strangers in a strange land.

But Sebastian was home. And he wasn't.

But a place to plant roots wasn't the issue at hand—it was getting a handle on a possible lead. He smiled in a way that he knew left women and thieves feeling both intrigued and slightly uneasy. And if his hunch was right in this case, the two might just turn out to be mutually inclusive. "Please, why don't you go in first?" he offered, forcing Lauren to ease by him.

Strange, but in all the editorial meetings she had attended in this space, Lauren had never experienced the entryway as being too narrow for comfort. She eased her way through. "So you're from Italy originally?"

"I was born in Italy, but my parents moved here when I was ten," he said, following her into the room. He motioned to the chairs pushed into the long table. "Have a seat," he said, and she nodded, slipping into one on the opposite side. "My father was an aerospace engineer, and he worked for the government in Huntsville, Alabama." He waited for her to sit before unbuttoning the front of his suit jacket and lowering himself into a seat.

Lauren decided to let Sebastian be the one to dispense with the usual small talk and move on to the subject of Harry Nord. Playing the waiting game, she contented herself with looking at his large hands spread calmly on the surface of the table. Contented probably wasn't the right word.

Sinews formed ridges on his tanned skin, and his nails were bluntly cut, attesting to strength born of outdoor activity. He wore a small, gold signet ring on his left hand, nothing effeminate—no, not by a long shot—just kind of classy, understatedly sophisticated. She had an almost irresistible urge to touch him and feel the contrast between the smooth ring and the rugged power of the muscles in his hands.

Lauren cleared her throat. "That explains your accent and your command of English," she said and tucked her hands in her lap under the table. She didn't feel like having him stare at her chewed nails. Strange, but their gnawed appearance had never worried her when she'd been engaged. That should have been a tip-off right there.

"Yes, well, even before we moved to the States, my mother insisted I learn English." He coughed softly and covered his mouth. Then he lowered his hand again and drummed lightly on the table.

Maybe not so relaxed, after all.

"She was enamored of all things American—cheeseburgers, skyscrapers, baseball, Harrison Ford," he said.

"How unItalian of her—except for the Harrison Ford part, that is."

"Her enthusiasm was so great I can safely say I was the only kid in Poggibonsi whose mother asked him to turn the radio *up* when it was playing American music."

Lauren looked at him askance. "Really? Somehow I can't picture you humming along to Metallica."

"You'd be surprised." He rubbed his chin, his finger passing over the little cleft.

No, she guessed she wasn't surprised at all. There was something dangerous about him. She instinctively knew he was bad for her health, but somehow she was drawn perversely closer. It was like succumbing to eating that second donut. No, she corrected herself, it was potentially far worse than several hundred empty calories.

"But not you?"

Lauren blinked. "Me?"

"You weren't a heavy metal fan?"

She held up a hand in confession. "Strictly Motown. The Four Tops. The Supremes. Aretha Franklin's 'Respect' was my personal anthem."

He studied her. "I can see you standing on top of

your bed, belting out 'Ain't No Mountain High Enough.'"

"Actually, it was mostly in the bathroom, with my toothbrush as a microphone and my brother Carl pounding on the door to get in."

Sebastian grinned, and his eyes opened wide, making the contrast between the milky whites and the dark, rich irises all the more pronounced, like chocolate Hostess cupcakes with a vanilla crème center—only in reverse. Ah, she really had empty calories on the brain. No, she knew she had other things on the brain.

"You know," he said, still smiling and looking so, so appealing, "if you tell me stories like that, I'm almost inclined to believe you're innocent."

3

"BUT I *AM* INNOCENT," she protested. *I may be lusting in my heart,* she thought, *but I am innocent.* "Well, in a fashion," she amended.

Sebastian leaned closer and reached out. He gently cupped her hand in his and let his fingertips—with their rough calluses, Lauren couldn't help noticing—brush her palm. "We all know there's no such thing as innocent." He studied her closely. "Though heaven knows if anyone is, it could possibly be you."

The pulse in her wrist throbbed with an aching urgency. "It's the lip gloss," Lauren mumbled.

"Lip gloss?"

"It's pink. You see?" She raised her other hand and rested her index finger on her lower lip.

He stared. At her hand. At her extended finger. At her cherry-blossom-stained lips.

And she gazed at his chest. Time became measured by the rise and fall of his pectorals.

And then he turned his gaze and let go of her hand.

Lauren stared at the table and rapidly pulled her hand back into her lap. "Well, if nobody's innocent in your book, doesn't that mean you're not innocent, either?" she asked. She looked up defiantly.

He played with a gold cuff link.

And then it hit her. "Hey, if you're here to bilk the paper with some kind of con, you're talking to the wrong person. The *Sentinel* might be a two-bit rag, and Ray is a scumbag in every sense of the word, but that doesn't mean I'm about to help you commit a crime. In fact, I've pretty much decided the only honorable thing to do about this mess is to own up to the fact that I concocted the whole thing—Harry's childhood, his war record, the philanthropy. True, it was meant to be a little joke—"

Sebastian looked at her askance.

"All right, more than a joke. I was pissed at Ray, but then that's another story." She waved her hand. "In any case, I never meant for the story to go to print. But seeing as it did, I think it's only fair that I take responsibility."

He sat up straight. "I don't think so."

That stopped Lauren. "You don't think so?" She narrowed her eyes. He was deadly serious. "Who are you, anyway?"

"I'm an investigator for the European division of the World Organization for Retrieving Stolen Art. It's an international registry of looted works of art." Sebastian slipped a picture ID from the inside pocket of his suit jacket.

Lauren quickly scanned the card. She shook her head. "I'm still not clear about what you do."

"I recover stolen art. The commission has an Internet site that lists items of cultural value taken by thieves. Publishing this information as widely as possible gets the public involved and helps us retrieve the items. It's been very successful. Since

1999, we've recovered roughly four hundred and twenty works of art, and we have over seven thousand cases under investigation. At the moment, I'm working with the Italian Carabinieri Unit for the Defense of the Cultural Heritage, in the hopes of lowering that figure by four."

"Looted art? Italian police?" She held up both hands as if to motion stop. "What does this all have to do with me?"

"Possibly a great deal." He reached into the same pocket and pulled out a wallet-size photograph. He slid it across the table toward Lauren.

She inclined forward and picked it up. It was an old black-and-white snapshot of a man in uniform. Not a man really, more a kid, judging by his puppyish features and wide-eyed stare. And from the age of the photo and the vintage of the uniform, he was a babe in the woods who had served in World War II. She flipped it over but there was no identification on the back. She glanced up.

"Bernard Lord," Sebastian said in answer to her silent question.

"Bernard Lord?" Lauren frowned and looked at the photo again. "Sorry, it doesn't ring a bell." She placed the snapshot on the table.

Sebastian tilted his head. "Are you sure? Why not take another look? The photo's old, and there's a chance that you came into contact with him when he was older, much older."

Lauren glanced at the picture and shook her head. "No, neither the name nor the face mean anything to me."

Sebastian sat up straighter and crossed his arms.

"Bernard Lord was born in Camden eighty-three years ago. An orphan, his formal education was spotty at best. During World War II, he enlisted in the army and was assigned to the air corps. He was later shot down over northern Italy."

Lauren shook her head in disbelief. "That's amazing. If I didn't know better, I'd say Bernard Lord *was* Harry Nord. I mean, not the real Harry Nord, but my fake Harry Nord."

"You sure it was fake?" He stared without blinking.

"Of course I'm sure. I realize there are a number of coincidences—" She was feeling flustered and rubbed her hands together before planting them squarely on the table.

Sebastian uncrossed his arms and leaned forward. He joined his hands, a mirror image of hers. The photo of Bernard Lord rested halfway between them, a link. A bone of contention.

"Over the years, I've come to realize there is no such thing as coincidence."

Lauren gulped. "Maybe this is the exception to your rule?"

Sebastian pushed the photo closer to her clenched hands. "Sixteen years ago, Bernard Lord made a sizeable contribution to a small hill town in northern Italy, at least, sizable by the village's standards. Later the villagers discovered that while Lord giveth, he also taketh away." His smile was enigmatic.

Lauren shivered and shook her head. "I don't understand."

"It seems that on his visit to the town, Mr. Lord

may have also liberated a small but exquisite painting by Caravaggio from the church, in addition to a rare Carolingian silver chalice and a pair of marble candlesticks attributed to Nicola Pisano. The thefts were only discovered after his departure. And not only did he depart, he disappeared into thin air. Without any real proof, the townspeople couldn't pin the thefts on a man many still considered to be their benefactor. The case was only recently reopened when the local police chief retired, and the new one decided he should contact the Carabinieri. They, in turn, contacted me."

Lauren peered down at the photo of the young man whose skinny neck looked lost in his uniform collar. "Let me guess. The painting, the chalice and the candlesticks were worth more than his contribution?"

Sebastian nodded once. "Far more. And you're going to help me find them."

Lauren studied his serious expression. "But, like I said, I never met, I've never even heard of Bernard Lord. And the world of art and paintings hardly figures into my beat at the paper. How can I possibly help you?"

"For the past twenty-five years or so, Bernard Lord received his veteran's pension at a post office box in central Philadelphia. Approximately six months ago, he stopped cashing them. The police have no record of his whereabouts or death. I can only presume he stopped collecting them because he somehow got wind of my investigation." Sebastian paused. "As you possibly did, as well, either consciously or unconsciously incorporating it into your story on Harry Nord."

Lauren splayed her hands across the front of her sweater. "And what possible motive would I have for doing that?"

"I don't know. You tell me."

Lauren threw up her arms. "Why are you making me feel like the guilty party here? All right, I'm guilty of losing my temper and letting a prank get out of hand, but beyond that…" She narrowed her eyes. "Beyond that, if we're going to start casting aspersions, you're the one who came waltzing in, pretending to be Harry Nord's grandson. Wouldn't it have been simpler, needless to say, more truthful, just to come in and say what you really wanted? Why the whole deception?"

"Rather than deception, I prefer to think of it as discretion. In general, I find a low-key approach yields more information and limits further complications."

The light dawned. "Meaning nobody else, possibly me, making off with the goods before you can apprehend them?" She frowned in indignation.

Sebastian smiled. Lauren Jeffries probably didn't realize it, but when she was irritated, her pouting lips only added to the edgy attractiveness of her seemingly angelic face. An angelic face that appeared at odds with a criminal mentality.

But his gut told him there was a connection. In which case, she was more likely a fallen angel. Curiously, the image was somehow more compelling.

As long as he kept his eye on the prize, Sebastian figured he could also enjoy, to be a polite Southerner, certain fringe benefits. After all, he enjoyed women—without the least inclination or desire to develop emotional attachments, that is. His mother had taught him *that* lesson. And one thing was for sure—Lauren Jeffries was a tantalizing woman. Amazing, when you considered how that purple sweater she was wearing covered her from chin to waist. Still, try as it might, it couldn't hide her rounded breasts.

He leaned closer. "Let me tell you, darlin', apprehending you would give me no greater pleasure."

His remark should have horrified her. Irritated her at the very least. Instead, it left a tingly stranglehold playing havoc with her vocal cords and an awkward sensation between her legs that had nothing to do with her khakis cutting into her bottom.

She shifted in her seat. "I'm not sure pleasure is the operative word at the moment." Who was she kidding?

"Who are you trying to fool?" He gently snared one of her hands and enveloped it in the warmth of his. "Me or you?" He rubbed the pad of his thumb across the back of her palm.

Lauren sniffed loudly. That awkward feeling— the one that had her squirming—only got worse, worse in that achingly desirable way that could get a girl into real trouble. "As a reporter, I must confess I'm used to asking the questions, not answering them."

"Confessions are good. And I have my ways of bringing them out."

His words left the roof of her mouth burning. She found herself tilting forward, when the smart thing to do would have been to head straight for the hills or, barring that, the ladies' room, Tupperware party announcement and all. "Am I supposed to be scared? Will you pull out the handcuffs when I refuse to cooperate?"

Sebastian's smile only grew larger. "Trust me, there's no question about your cooperation." He bent forward, their heads now separated by a few crucial inches, drawn together by a force far greater than gravity. "And it won't take restraints." He angled his head.

She stared at his broad mouth and full lower lip. "It won't?" Her voice was low, breathy.

Sebastian brushed the photo aside and reached to cup her jaw. "Not unless you want it to."

And he lowered his head and kissed her, teasing her lips with the heat of his, drawing her nearer so that she had to place a hand on his shoulder or she'd fall.

But she did anyway—into the best, most sensual kiss of her life. A kiss that had her thinking how good he was at this, and how turned on she was by the rough abrasion of his teeth against her lips and the playful but purposeful dance of his tongue around the contours of her mouth. And how his doing all this made her *stop* thinking completely and let the overwhelming sensation of feeling grip her totally. Where they were and what was going on around them became a vague blur, an amorphous ambience against which she tasted and touched the one thing that seemed alive.

Until he abruptly pulled away.

And Lauren would have banged her nose, but good, on the table if the voice from hell hadn't penetrated her cloudy consciousness.

"So it's all settled then?" Ray popped his large head through the door.

Lauren gripped the edge of the table.

Sebastian rose and smoothed his dark blue tie. If the kiss affected him, he wasn't letting on. "I think so. Ms. Jeffries has agreed to my idea."

Lauren froze. "I have?" She eyed him suspiciously.

Ray came around to the head of the table and stared earnestly at Lauren. "Now, I want you to do me proud, kid. I intended to have someone senior do the feature, but seeing as you'd already filed the obit on his grandfather, Mr. Alberti insisted that you were the right person for the assignment."

Lauren rose slowly. "Let me get this straight. You want me to write a feature on Harry Nord?"

"Not that you won't still be responsible for your regular beat—and the obits, of course. I'm not running a country club here. But if you do a good job, I may even bump the story out of Metro," Ray said magnanimously. Lauren could tell he was feeling magnanimous because he put his hand inside his belt buckle and rubbed it back and forth.

"I would think that the scope of the story could easily raise the newspaper's and the reporter's profiles quite dramatically." Sebastian gazed at Lauren from beneath his dark brows.

So that's where all this was coming from. Sebastian had convinced Ray that she should work on a bigger story on Harry Nord because it had higher circulation—and maybe even Pulitzer—written all over it. Meanwhile, he'd stick to her like glue with the idea that she'd crack and divulge her involvement with Bernard Lord.

Well, there was nothing to crack on that score. But if Bernard Lord still *did* live in the area, she was sure she could track him down. Once she got on the trail of a story, she didn't quit until she landed the goods. And besides, all those years of attending the local Catholic schools had left her with more than the usual social maladjustments—it also meant she knew half of Philly's police force. If anyone was going to break open the case, it was she. In which case, there really *was* potential news value. And a chance to move out of Metro—way out.

She turned her full wattage of charm on Ray. "Just remember to carve out six inches above the fold on Page One by the end of next week."

Ray, momentarily stunned that she wasn't affording him her usual scowl—and no doubt shocked by her display of chutzpah—forgot to breathe. "Page One?" Ray removed his hand from his belt. His face turned a sickening puce before he recovered. "You're right. The whole 'This is your life' scenario has real appeal. Maybe we'll throw some advertising behind it, as well."

Lauren smiled brightly and caught Sebastian's pleased expression out of the corner of her eye. And realized almost immediately that he'd fooled someone other than Ray. Sebastian Alberti had counted on her being blinded by the lure of a terrific story, that is, if he was giving her the benefit of the doubt. There was still the issue of his thinking she was somehow involved in the thefts, and that she would have to play along if she was going to get him off her back.

Either way, he had her. But it could be like having a tiger by its tail. Because if she let things run their course and wasn't successful at uncovering Bernard Lord and the stolen loot, she'd never be able to atone for the mess she'd caused. It would be an absolute kiss of death.

Why hadn't she thought of that when she'd locked lips with Sebastian Alberti? She could still call a halt to the proceedings now and fess up to the obit prank. That way she might have a chance of salvaging her career. Slim, but nevertheless a chance. "Ray?" She looked up, prepared to bite the bullet. "About Harry Nord…"

"You can rest assured," Sebastian quickly interrupted, "we won't let my grandfather stay buried."

Ray punched the air. He could have been Robert Preston leading the band in *The Music Man*. "You'll keep her on track, Mr. Alberti. I can see that. Meanwhile, I gotta run. Seems it wasn't a hijacking at the State House, but a catering truck that rammed into a van of rabbis. All we know so far is that four of them were covered in lobster Newburg. We've got a call into the theological seminary to see if that violates any kosher regulations."

Lauren watched Ray's retreating figure. She felt as if a catering truck had hit her, as well. She slowly swiveled around on the wooden heel of one clog and faced Sebastian. "I guess I should thank you for getting me Page One on a story that involves investigating someone who doesn't even exist."

"That's not necessary. In any case, we both know that if you can uncover the scoop on the real Harry Nord, aka Bernard Lord, you'll be filing a far bigger story." He paused and added almost impulsively,

"Besides, look at the positive side. Working together will help to cement an amicable, ongoing relationship."

"Amicable, ongoing relationship?" Lauren felt a ripple of dread mixed with excitement curl in her stomach and travel helter-skelter to her throat.

"Yes, you heard Ray. I'm supposed to keep you on track."

"Please, I have a very good sense of direction. And I think things would move far more efficiently if I did the legwork myself and got back to you with daily updates by phone or, if you insist, in person at the office. Trust me, it's not as if I'm going to skip town."

Sebastian stepped around the table. "I don't think so."

Lauren willed herself not to back up when he halted next to her. Very close next to her. Close enough that she could practically measure within a few degrees the angles of his prominent cheekbones, not to mention inhale another whiff of his subtle, woodsy aftershave. Yes, she'd definitely prefer not to mention that.

She cleared her throat. "And why is it you don't trust me?"

Sebastian studied her lips. "Well, among other things, I think it's got something to do with your pink lip gloss."

There was a moment of silence, after which Sebastian walked to the conference room doorway and waited for her to pass—ever the gentleman. "So where do we start?"

Somehow, etiquette didn't seem to have anything to do with his proposition.

4

LAUREN MADE NO EFFORT to hide her scowl as she turned to lead the way to her desk. "The Metro section is over in the back corner." She clomped swiftly down the hall without bothering to look back to see if he was keeping up. If he got lost, so much the better. Sebastian Alberti gave her the willies. No, he gave her more than that. He made every nerve ending in her body acutely aware of things like the smell of hazelnut-flavored coffee and quiet desperation wafting up the stairwell from the Classified section. Ad space was down, and the hazelnut coffee was probably a contributing factor.

Lauren took a sharp right past the City Hall desk and knew instantly he was still following. Closely. Her scalp prickled with the subtle rise in temperature.

This was not good, definitely not good. She lengthened her stride, unaware that the exaggerated gait left a lasting impression for anyone with a view from behind.

Needless to say, Sebastian was as observant as the next man. Maybe even more, given his professional training and artistically inclined eye. An eye that normally lumped women who wore those ridiculous wooden shoes in the company of plow horses, but in this case looked charmingly contrapuntal against Lauren's energized strides and nicely rounded rear end. He pursed his lips and watched her take the corner past a low partition with the skill of a professional driver. Yes, definitely a nicely rounded rear end.

Life could be a lot worse, he reflected with the sardonic smile that seemed as much a part of his being as his fingers and toes. How often did he get the excuse to follow a woman who attracted him as much as Lauren Jeffries? She appeared to be a fragile doll, her cap of pale blond hair haloing her delicate features. Yet she was as tough as nails, with the ramrod-straight posture of a bantamweight boxer. And that mouth of hers. Her quick, Northeastern way of speaking with its sarcastic bite. Ah, yes, that mouth. He thought of her full, blushing-pink lips.... He coughed and adjusted his steps as she slowed down.

Lauren stopped at a small cubicle demarcated by low beige fabric-covered walls. The only thing that distinguished it from the other work areas in the cavernous room was a "Metro" nameplate affixed at the opening. Her own name occupied the slot directly below, while the third slot was empty.

"It's a little cramped, but you can sit there if you want." She pointed to an empty swivel chair. A counter, which served as a continuous desktop, lined three sides of the cubicle. In addition to two computers and phones, there were dual In and Out baskets. "Frankly, I wouldn't go near it without a serious dose of Lysol and an incantation from a voodoo priest. But then, I'm not the most trusting of people."

"Any particular reason?"

"For my naturally suspicious nature?"

"Actually, I was referring to the desk chair, but your point is perhaps more interesting."

Lauren scowled. "Trust me, there's nothing interesting along that line. As to the chair, it used to be Baby Huey's."

"Baby Huey?" Sebastian raised his eyebrows in question.

Very nice, slightly arched black brows, Lauren couldn't help noticing. She cleared her throat. "Huey Neumeyer, the new State House reporter?"

Sebastian nodded. "Ah, yes—the lobster Newburg incident. I can see how that could generate a lot of reader interest." He glanced at the empty chair. "I take it he worked in the Metro department until recently?"

Lauren maneuvered her foot around one caster of her chair and pulled it out to sit down. "That's putting it politely. Huey finds breathing through his nose a full-time activity. In any case, his computer and phone are still functioning. I can just plug in my password, so if you need to check into your office, go right ahead."

"That's all right. I carry my office with me." He slipped a wafer-thin PDA from his inside breast pocket.

"Next time the *Sentinel* has a few grand they want to throw my way, I'll know what to ask for. In the meantime, I'll have to make do with one of these." She picked up a steno pad from her desk, then turned to boot up her computer.

Sebastian didn't take her dismissal personally—he didn't take anything in life personally. Instead, he seized the opportunity to look freely at Lauren's workspace and glean some information about her.

In contrast to the barren bulletin board over the other desk, Lauren's was packed with a *Far Side* wall calendar, phone lists, birthday cards and photos. There was a school photo of a little girl missing a front tooth. And almost hidden beneath a snapshot of a baby staring wide-eyed from the lap of a redheaded woman was a picture of Lauren and the Amazonian Phoebe, a true Mutt and Jeff combination if ever there was one. They were grinning into the camera and holding plastic cups of what looked like red wine. Behind them, a conference room was decked out in tacky holiday decorations—a recent Christmas party at the newspaper, no doubt. Lauren had her blond hair in pigtails, a fuzzy red scarf wrapped around her neck and high color on her cheeks.

By all rights she should have looked like a somewhat tipsy Heidi, but Sebastian's thoughts were hardly on Swiss orphans. Instead he found himself internally yodeling the delights of slowly disrobing her, leaving only the scarlet boa, and slipping the bands from her hair one by one so that the silky tresses fanned over her cheeks and onto a pillow....

Sebastian blinked. It was happening again, this completely uncharacteristic loss of focus. He cleared his throat and frowned, concentrating on her fingers moving rapidly over the keyboard. "Is that something to do with the case?" He peered over her shoulder.

Lauren swiveled her neck and glanced up. Sebastian loomed over her shoulder like a vulture—a very sexy vulture, but a vulture nonetheless. "I was planning on accessing LexisNexis. Didn't you want to sit over there and play with your BlackBerry or something?"

"Well, you did warn me about the chair. Besides, it's not every day I get to see a newspaperwoman in action."

Lauren rolled her eyes but decided it was best to ignore him—well, at least pretend to ignore him.

She pulled up the search engine that served as the research bible for journalists and typed in Harry Nord's name, plus Philadelphia, in an attempt to winnow down the number of hits. The obituary she'd fabricated immediately popped up. But right below it was a second item from 1950: a sidebar to a story in the Sports section on Game Two of the World Series between Philadelphia and New York. After a disappointing loss to the Yankees on a homer by DiMaggio, it seems a distraught Harry Nord was in a car accident while driving home from Shibe Park—the Phillies old stomping grounds. Nord's wife, the only other member of Nord's family, was killed, and he was left completely paralyzed.

"If Nord became a quadriplegic over fifty years ago, I don't see him travelling back to Italy after the fact, let alone heisting any art treasures. *Your* Bernard Lord must be a completely different guy. Let's see what we get on Bernard Lord instead," she said out loud, and absentmindedly scratched her neck as she waited for the search to finish.

Sebastian stared at her small hand exposing the white skin at the nape of her neck and had a definite urge to push her fingers aside and run his own across her smooth skin. He breathed in, telling himself to ignore the light scent of lavender. "Do you really think you need to type in Bernard Lord's name?"

She dropped her hand to her lap. "Are you implying that if I'm really Bernard Lord's accomplice, I would know everything already? Please, even if I were in on the thefts, you'd think I'd be stupid enough not to pretend otherwise?"

"You'd be surprised how stupid most people are."

She peered at the screen as the information came up. "I'm not most people."

"I figured that," he murmured and leaned next to her ear to read over her shoulder. The smell of her gentle soap was stronger, invitingly stronger. He willed himself to study the screen. While he didn't have access to this particular data bank, his own tie-in to Interpol was far from shabby. Still, if there was one thing he had learned over the years, any information was relevant—even a dead end.

That's why when he'd seen the wire story on Harry Nord's purported obit he decided to follow through. And his instincts told him that he might have gotten lucky. How lucky, he didn't quite know.

"Hmm," she mumbled. "Seems your Bernard Lord was quite a flyboy after all—Bronze Star, Purple Heart. Nothing new as far as you're concerned, though. Let's see what else we can get—maybe through the Veteran's Administration." She tapped in a cross-reference. "No, nothing interesting there."

Sebastian rested a hand on the back of her chair. "Why don't you try Camden?"

Lauren poised her fingers on the keyboard. "Camden? As in New Jersey?"

"That's right. You wrote in the obit that that was where Harry Nord was born."

Lauren frowned. "That's right. But it was something I made up, if I remember my notes correctly. Still, it's just across the river, so why not?" She shrugged and typed in the information. And while the computer hummed away, she tucked her fine hair behind her ear, inches from his face.

Sebastian watched her gesture and was suddenly conscious of the delicate curve of her ear. It would be so easy for him to lower his head and nuzzle her lobe. Offer a teasing bite. Cause Lauren to turn her head and offer more than a gentle nibble in return. More like a full-blown kiss on those plump lips… He gripped the chair more tightly.

"Bingo!" Lauren grabbed the steno pad and scribbled notes. "Seems a Bernard Lord reported a break-in at his apartment at 38 Roebling Street, Collingswood, eight years ago." She moved her head back and forth as she scanned the copy. "Missing items included a silver tea set, Lenox china. Gee, pretty pricey items for that neck of the woods. Wait a minute—" she scrolled back up "—Roebling Street. That rings a bell somehow."

She swiveled her chair a few degrees, forcing Sebastian to let go, and rifled through a stack of papers on her desk. "I must have left it here some place." Coming up empty-handed, she flipped through another, then pulled out a drawer with a stack of steno pads. She ducked her head and searched.

"Looking for something?" Sebastian joined her by the open drawer.

She lifted the top few pads and went through them one at a time. "Yeah, my notes on Harry Nord. I took down information from the press release from the funeral parlor and the VA hospital to write up a 'real' obit, which of course, I never actually did when all the hoopla broke out. I must have it here somewhere."

He stared at the jumble of notebooks. "Maybe I could help you look? Otherwise we could be here until it's time for you to collect your pension."

"Technically, the *Sentinel* has a K1 plan, not a pension plan, which, because I've been here four years already—" she stopped going through the pads and blinked. "I can't believe it's already been four years." She shook her head. "Never mind. If I think about that too much I'll go into a terminal funk. What were we looking for— Oh, right, the notes on Harry Nord. Sure, I suppose you can help look. Just grab a handful. My filing system might not be the greatest, but at least you'll see I carefully mark the cover with the dates that I used the pad and what stories the notes refer to. See, this one says 'Christmas Tree Scam', 'Homeless Shelters Revving Up For Winter Weather', 'Soup Kitchens Facing Shortage Of Food.'"

She skimmed through the pages. "Everybody thinks the holidays are so great, but for some people, it's just more hardship. At least the story on the soup kitchen generated some interest—they called me to let me know a supermarket chain made a large donation in response. Kind of makes the beat worthwhile after all."

She closed the notebook and for the first time glanced over at Sebastian and noticed that he was staring at her. His mouth, that incredibly sensuous mouth, was slightly open, and the top ridge of his bottom teeth exposed. "What? Do I have something on my nose or something?" She reached up but didn't feel anything more than the little bump on one side, the result of having fallen out of the top bunk at a sleepover party when she was nine. Her mother was forever suggesting that she apply concealer to mask it.

"It's not so much your nose as your eyes, your expression. You don't even realize how you telegraph every emotion—frustration, modesty, pride, tenderness." Sebastian studied her some more, shifting his head first one way and then the other.

Wow, frustration, modesty, pride—let alone tenderness—were not the emotions that immediately came to the fore. And if he could read her thoughts that easily, well, he'd figured out that embarrassment was following hard on the heels of lust. "I guess I shouldn't play poker then," she stammered.

"You also shouldn't delve into crime. I'll catch you, you know?" He moved his head more closely to hers. The width of the drawer the measure of separation.

"What if I don't want to be caught?" She wasn't talking about crime.

"There's a theory that deep down, all criminals secretly want to be caught, you know."

"But I'm not a criminal," she protested, intent on the movement of his full lips.

"Then I'll just have to further my investigation to confirm that, won't I?" He tilted closer and angled his mouth.

Lauren bit her top lip and let go, opening her mouth in breathless anticipation. The notebook in her hands tumbled atop the others.

"So this is how you follow up on a story!" The squeaky exclamation was followed up with a loud snort.

Flustered, Lauren jerked herself upright, banging her shoulder on the edge of her desk. She rubbed the sore spot. "Huey, I'm surprised to find you slumming around the Metro section. You need me to tie your shoes before you head out the door on your big seafood scoop?"

Huey scowled, causing a few more flakes of dandruff to join the blizzard that adorned the shoulders of his too-tight blazer. They resembled sprinkles on a cupcake. "You know, you should be nicer to me. I have influence. I can make life difficult for you around here."

"What are you going to do, Huey?" She emphasized his name. "Jam the photocopier the way you usually do?" Lauren shot back. She was beyond worrying about retribution. What was Ray going to do? Demote her to making coffee? She did that anyway.

"I don't need to be insulted," Huey retorted.

"Then why don't you leave? In case you haven't figured it out, you're not entirely wanted around here. And trust me, it's not just professional."

She glanced down at the drawer, which of course immediately reminded her of the kiss that almost was. An almost-kiss that had left her breathless in a way that far exceeded even the three-hour necking session at the postprom party her senior year in high school. She shook her head and stared at the notebooks before reluctantly turning to Huey. "You haven't seen a pad of mine lying around, have you, maybe when you were clearing out your desk last week? It's got my notes on Harry Nord."

Huey screwed up his close-set eyes. Not a pretty sight. "This is a new low, even for you. Just because I got a promotion and you didn't, you accuse me of stealing your work?"

"You're right, what was I thinking?" She banged her forehead with her palm. "You wouldn't know what to do with my notes even if I dictated you a story from them. Now that I think about it, I must have taken the notebook home that evening, just jammed it into my bag. It's probably sitting on my dining table along with my unpaid Visa bill. I apologize profusely for my unwarranted accusations."

"Well, if you put it that way." Huey appeared temporarily mollified. "Besides which, I only stopped by because Ray asked me to tell you he wants you in his office. Seems the fire department put out a warning about the dangers of low water pressure in the hydrants, and Ray wants a story."

Lauren sighed. "I can see the lead now. 'Kiddies, don't open fire hydrants in the warm weather, no matter how much fun it could be.' I'm surprised you didn't grab at the chance to write up that one."

"I have bigger fish to fry now that I'm the State

House reporter." Huey thrust his shoulders back, an unfortunate gesture given that the button straining against his round waistline finally gave way and popped across the cubicle.

Sebastian efficiently bent over and retrieved it. He held it out. "Actually, I was under the impression that lobster Newburg was simmered, not fried."

Huey snatched at the button and hustled out of the cubicle as quickly as his Easy Spirits could take him.

Sebastian looked at Lauren, who had risen out of her chair and was busy opening another drawer and grabbing her shoulder bag. "You think it's smart to bait him that way?" he asked.

"What's he going to do? Go running to Ray complaining I don't play nice?" Her head was buried in her bag as she pushed through its contents. "Even if he is the boss's relative, there's no way Ray is going to fire me because that little pipsqueak asks him to. It's a simple matter of economics. No fresh-faced kid out of journalism school is going to settle for a salary as low as mine. When I was on the job market, I was so eager to get the position that I would have been willing to take less than the going rate at McDonald's. Come to think of it, I did." She rose and took a few more pens out of the can on her desk, which was decorated with a decoupage of grocery store coupons past their expiration dates. The den mother of Lauren's niece's Brownie troop had a lot to answer for.

She slung the strap of her purse over her shoulder then stopped. "On second thought, you hold on to this." She thrust the envelope-shaped Coach bag in Sebastian's direction. Phoebe had talked her into buying it at an end-of-season sale. Even at thirty percent off, it had been beyond her budget. Lauren should have known not to go shopping after drinking two glasses of wine.

Sebastian stared at the bag. "You want me to hold your purse?"

"I want you to stay here and hold my bag while I stop in at Ray's office to get this hydrant assignment. Then I'll have time to slip out and get my notes from my apartment. There's something about Roebling Street in Camden that rings a bell."

"Sorry if I'm a little dense, but why am I the designated purse holder? If it's to test my masculine security, I can assure you it's quite intact." Sebastian held up her bag.

Lauren breathed in deeply. "Somehow I'm not surprised. But to answer your question, you're holding it because I want to sneak out, and Ray will put up a stink if he thinks I'm bailing out on a rinky-dink public service piece in favor of a potential Pulitzer prize story." She held up her hand. "And, yes, before you ask, his priorities *are* that skewed. Besides—" she gave him an endearing smile that caused more than a little excitement in Sebastian's nether regions "—*you* were the one who wanted to develop a close working relationship, correct?"

Sebastian cleared his throat. "As long as I'm not caught holding the bag."

UNFORTUNATELY, RAY WAS in one of his expansive let-me-explain-to-you-the-meaning-of-journalism-not-to-mention-life moods. His sentences invariably began with the words "Now in my day…" Rather than suffer through the arcane details of Ray's experiences as a cub reporter in the Precambrian era, Lauren finally grabbed the press release from the fire department and hightailed it out of his office with the excuse, "I'll be sure to get this in the Monday edition, but it's that time of the month, and I really do need to go to the ladies' room."

Ray blinked and let her go immediately.

Clumping down the hallway as fast as her legs would go, Lauren glanced down at her watch. "Great, a twenty-minute discourse on the glory days of Edward R. Murrow." She turned the corner without looking up and barely had time to stop herself from ramming directly into Sebastian.

Even still, she had to rock back on her heels to reclaim her balance. Actually, she was starting to come to the conclusion that she was permanently off balance when it came to being around Sebastian Alberti. Especially when he did things like smile slyly and greet her with, "Darlin', this way of meeting is becoming a habit."

Lauren crossed her arms in front of her chest. She had the suspicion the sudden strain on her lace bra was not due to the effects of dry skin. "Well, maybe if you didn't stand like some sequoia in the middle of traffic it wouldn't happen so often."

"Don't worry that you've offended me," he said, watching her grab a worn leather jacket from a hook.

"Some things worry me, but offending you is not

one of them." She slipped on the coat. "Good, you've got my bag, too. I'll take it now. If we walk quickly we should be able to get to my place in thirty minutes or so." She marched to the elevators and raised her hand to punch the Down button.

His left hand was there first. She rubbed her forehead and tried not to be pleased at the lack of a wedding ring. She studied the lighted Down button with keen interest.

"You know, I'm truly flattered that you think of me as firmly thrusting myself upwards," he said with that mischievous lilt of his.

Lauren instantly looked up. "What on earth are you talking about?" The elevator opened and she got in and plastered herself against the back wall—as far away from Sebastian as possible.

Sebastian calmly joined her, leaning forward to push the lobby floor button before resting his back next to hers. "Your choice of words? Calling me a sequoia?"

Lauren gazed heavenwards. "That was just a figure of speech."

He smiled slyly. "Ah, but you above all people know the power of words."

The elevator stopped at the next floor. "Hi, Lauren, going out?" asked a female voice.

Lauren tilted her head down and saw that Donna Drinkwater, the doyenne of the supply closet, had joined them. And while Donna had addressed the question to her, her eyes—with their pale orange lashes—were zeroed in on Sebastian. Lauren would have dearly loved to shake Donna by her ample shoulders—despite being only five foot two, Donna had a real shot at a linebacker position on the Eagles—and tell her, "Donna, you're old enough to be his maiden aunt and besides, why don't you stop wearing crocheted vests that make you look like an afghan rug?"

"Donna," Lauren instead said politely, "I don't think you've met our celebrity guest, Sebastian Alberti." Donna smiled sweetly, and Lauren could almost forgive her the crocheted vests—no, she couldn't. "Sebastian, this is Donna Drinkwater, an invaluable member of the staff and one of the few people who actually has Engelbert Humperdinck's phone number."

"Engelbert Humperdinck?" Sebastian asked with raised brows.

"You know, the seventies singer with the big sideburns that came all the way down his jaw?" Lauren mimicked the effect.

Sebastian opened his mouth, but he needed a moment to get the words out. "Of course, Engelbert Humperdinck. Without question, his rivals, Tom Jones and Julio Iglesias, pale in comparison." All this, and he managed a straight face.

Then Sebastian took Donna's hand and for a moment, Lauren thought he was going to kiss it. Instead he gently shook hands and Donna, still in a daze, let hers drop limply back to her side. Lauren wondered if Donna would avoid washing it for days.

Whatever. Lauren was eternally grateful that they reached the lobby without anybody else getting on. "It was a pleasure meeting you, Donna," Sebastian said in parting. "And I must tell you,

Engelbert Humperdinck's rendition of 'Release Me' has always been one of my favorites."

Donna slumped in the corner. "If you send me your e-mail address, I'll be sure to include you in the fan mail listing." She weakly raised her hand.

Lauren walked swiftly across the lobby to the bank of glass doors. "'Release Me?' Puh-lease. Do you always have to lay it on so thick?"

"You wanted me to tell Donna that the last decent crooner was Perry Como? I don't think so." His large strides easily caught up with her choppy steps. "There's no need to rush, you know."

"I thought you were as anxious as I am to get to the bottom of the Bernard Lord story." She pushed through the revolving door. "We've already lost a lot of the day due to Ray's penchant for verbal diarrhea. And you know, it's going to take a while to walk to my place."

"That's what I thought, so I brought the car around to the front while you were occupied."

Lauren stopped on the sidewalk. "But there's no parking in front of the building."

Sebastian withdrew his car keys from his trouser pocket. "Maybe for some people, but the security guard assured me I'd have no problem."

Lauren looked at him in disgust. "Do you always get your way?"

Sebastian humored her by actually pausing to think a moment. "Yes, I'd say so." He nodded in the direction of the curb. "So how about you getting in the car before I pull out my gun?"

"You really carry a gun? I wouldn't think your tailoring would allow it." Lauren glanced in the general vicinity of his waist, and for the first time she realized that there might be times when a stolen art inspector did more than analyze flakes of paint. "Okay, I get the message." She held up her hand. "Home, Jeeves."

5

IT TOOK A MOMENT FOR the crowd of pedestrians to pass and give Lauren a clear shot at making it to the curb. When she did, she let out a low whistle. A black Mercedes SLK gleamed in the April sun. "Do international art theft investigators work on a commission or something?"

"Let's just say I like toys."

"I just bet you do. In your line of work I'm sure you get to use all types of macho gadgets—X-ray lasers, paper chromatographs. Who knows, maybe even Hummers painted in artistic camouflage colors—you know, to blend in with the stolen Raphaels and Michelangelos."

Sebastian raised an eyebrow. "Actually, I much prefer my tractor painted in classic John Deere green."

That gave Lauren pause. "Tractor? What do you do—furrow for clues?"

Sebastian grabbed the sides of his suit jacket and buttoned the middle button with greater care than Lauren thought was strictly necessary. "It's for personal use."

Lauren frowned. "You need a tractor in D.C.?"

Sebastian's head came up quickly. "What makes you say D.C.?"

Lauren rolled her eyes. "Oh, brother, talk about suspicious. You probably don't even trust your own mother."

He didn't hesitate. "I don't." His voice was flat.

And Lauren didn't think he was joking. She raised her hand to say something, but let it drop to her side. "I guessed you lived in D.C. because your ID card listed your organization as based there, and because the plates on your car come from the District. Okay?" She casually waved in the general direction of the bumper. "Should we get going then?"

Sebastian unlocked the car doors and opened the passenger side. "I'm surprised you didn't drive yourself today. Early spring mornings can still be mighty chilly."

She slipped into the leather seat. "Well, it's like this, if I don't walk, I take the bus."

"You take the bus?" He sounded aghast. He was aghast.

Lauren turned to face him as he got in on the driver's side. "I have my eye on the new Jaguar, but unfortunately the dealer is back-ordered on the color I want." Lauren shook her head. "Of course, I take the bus. On what the paper pays me, I'm lucky that I have my own place and don't have to live with my parents anymore."

"And that irks you? The low salary?"

"Money wasn't what motivated me to become a reporter. It was finding the truth, informing people to help them have a better grasp of the world and make more informed voting choices. And I wanted to be able to give them insight into their neighbors in order to build a sense of community and be touched in a unique way." She held up only to catch her breath.

"Thank you, Woodward and Bernstein. But the money irks you, right?" He rested his hands on the steering wheel.

"Of course it irks me. I'd like to hit the end-of-season sales at Asta De Blue as much as the next gal, but I've learned to tamp down my fashionista urges and live within my means."

Sebastian surveyed her clothes slowly. Though Lauren thought he was surveying something else, along the lines of her less-than-generous breasts and somewhat too-rounded hips. "Yes, I noticed," he said as he let his gaze travel back to her face. "But there are other urges that have nothing to do with fashion, you know?"

Lauren pursed her lips. She really did not want to parse the meaning of "urges"—not sitting within easy lap-straddling distance of the most delectable man she had ever seen on this side of the silver screen.

And then it hit her—he wasn't talking about sex. She spun around and shot him a furious stare. "Listen, I'm not so strapped for cash that I would succumb to the urge—or whatever you call it—to steal priceless works of art which are near and dear to a small town's heritage. I am really growing tired of these innuendos, and I don't know what I can do to convince you that we're on the same side."

Sebastian studied her with a steady gaze.

Lauren refused to flinch. "Well?"

He wet his lips.

She stopped breathing, momentarily mesmerized, seemingly a contradiction in terms given that she was frustrated as hell with him at the same time.

He stilled his tongue on the ridge of his teeth, allowing Lauren to surmise that he was just as aware as she that the temperature in the car had suddenly risen, despite the careful monitoring by the Mercedes' computer.

Finally he shut his mouth and swallowed, breaking his hold on Lauren and allowing her to turn away. "Maybe if you pointed me in the right direction of the thief, you wouldn't be a suspect," he offered.

She slanted him a glance and held out a finger. No, not that finger—her index finger. "In that case, get in the left lane after you pull away from the curb, and I'll tell you when to turn."

IF IT WEREN'T FOR THE traffic, Sebastian and Lauren could have made it to her place on Pine Street in ten minutes. But that was like saying if the dog hadn't stopped to take a leak, he would have won the race.

Traffic jams were as much a part of Philadelphia as bodily functions were to canines.

The only thing worse than the traffic was the parking. Lauren directed Sebastian to one of the parking garages near Pennsylvania Hospital. From there, it was a short walk to the narrow brick row house where her top floor apartment was located. The recently renovated, well, partially renovated building—the landlord ran out of money before installing either the luxury bathrooms or granite countertops in the kitchens—exuded historical charm. Which was a good thing since the building to the left had a For Lease sign stuck at an angle on a boarded-up window. The building on the right had a sign more parallel to the pavement.

Sebastian stared up at the purple lettering and read out loud, "Elwood's Tattoos and Piercings. I see the neighborhood really attracts the most refined of businesses." He eyed her askance.

"I like to think we're on the cutting edge here in our little part of the world. Two blocks to the east is Society Hill. A couple in the other direction is Antiques Row. And don't knock Elwood. He promised to give me a discount on getting my belly button pierced."

Sebastian dropped his eyes. "And did you?"

Lauren frowned. "Did I what? Oh, you mean get my belly button pierced? Are you kidding me? Do you know how much my mother would freak out? It's bad enough that I moved out on my own."

"Your mother holds that much sway over your life?"

"Whose mother doesn't?" Lauren dug around in her bag for her house keys, not really expecting an answer.

She didn't get one. In any case, the noise of an ambulance whizzing past provided a temporary distraction. Sebastian watched it turn into the hospital. "How convenient for you and Elwood," he said. "And noisy."

"You get used to it. Besides, if I ever need an ambulance, they know where to find me."

"I'm sure that's a real selling point for luring prospective tenants."

"Be smug all you want. I'm proud to live here,"

Lauren retorted and turned to put her key in the front door lock. "That's weird."

Sebastian moved behind her. "What's weird?"

She swiveled around to look at him. Standing on the top of the marble stoop, she was eye to eye with him. "The door. It's unlocked."

He took the two steps in one stride and stood next to her. "You want me to go in first?"

Gee, having her own mysterious and sexy personal protector was like something out of a rerun of *The Highlander*. Lauren shook her head. Sebastian did not wear his hair in a ponytail, so she was safe. All right, it was raven black, but she could still deal with him and whatever was going on in her building.

"That's okay," she assured him, laying a hand on his arm to quell his protective instincts. Actually, that wasn't the best idea she'd had lately. Lauren never realized how even the most casual contact with rock-hard biceps could be so discombobulating. She whipped back her hand before she started doing something she'd regret—like yanking off his jacket and applying her lips to the pulse point on his wrist.

"Are you sure?" she heard him ask. And if Lauren didn't know better, she'd have sworn his rich baritone was a little tighter than usual.

She purposely avoided looking up, which was probably a good thing for a girl intent on regaining her composure. Otherwise she'd have noticed that the pupils of his eyes had dilated and his jaw was working overtime. But she hadn't.

Instead, she concentrated on the tips of her clogs

and stammered, "You know what?" Her brain finally clued in to information not tied to her libido. "Probably someone was just carrying a whole bunch of things in and out and forgot to flip the lock back on."

Sebastian raised a doubting eyebrow, but deferred to her judgment and let Lauren go through the door first. Since she could no longer stare at him, he actually had the chance to collect his composure.

From where in God's name had that protective he-man urge sprung? For a minute back there he'd felt like Rambo, ready to charge into the fray, and the next—when she'd laid her hand on his sleeve— he'd just about thrown her to the ground and had his way with her on the marble steps. Steps that really needed polishing, but not in a way that involved the type of activities he had in mind.

Jeez, for a man who prided himself on staying in control, analyzing situations and sizing people up, he suddenly seemed prone to rabid emotional impulses where Lauren Jeffries was concerned. It was one thing to indulge in extracurricular activities. It was quite another when they got in the way of your concentration.

Sebastian drew his brows together in a deep V and followed Lauren up the narrow stairway. She lived on the third floor of the building, and he had a prime view of her rear end in her khaki trousers as he followed several steps behind. With each lift of her leg, the material stretched across her rounded cheeks, allowing him to deduce in no uncertain terms that she wore thong panties.

He swallowed. With difficulty. *Concentrate*, he told himself.

Lauren trudged up the final flight of stairs and breathed through her mouth as she reached her apartment door. She'd moved in less than three weeks ago, and the trek upstairs was getting marginally better each time she came back. She reached up to unlock her door—but this time, Sebastian was the one to lay his hand on her.

"Don't." He uttered the one word in a whisper. He nodded toward her door, and Lauren saw for the first time that it was slightly ajar. She froze. "Go down the stairs and dial 911 on your cell phone," he said, his voice low.

Lauren gulped, telling herself now was not the time to panic. "I don't have a cell phone."

"A single women living alone in a city and you don't own a cell phone?" He shook his head. "Never mind. Use mine." He removed his hand from her sleeve and slipped it inside his coat. He held out the phone.

Lauren reached for it, aware that her hand shook. "And what are you planning on doing? Reenacting the 'Charge of the Light Brigade'?"

"Don't worry. I can handle myself." He moved his hand under his jacket to the small of his back.

Lauren didn't think he was reaching for a comb. "Great. Just great. You decide to play hero and possibly get yourself shot." Amazing how a little irritation could diminish fear.

Sebastian removed his arm from under his coat and grabbed her by both shoulders, summarily turning her around. "Will you go downstairs?" He thought he'd exercised amazing restraint by not kicking her in the butt.

Lauren scowled over her shoulder. "All right, I get the point. But no getting yourself killed and ruining my chances for the biggest story of my career, you hear?"

"And here I thought you were concerned for my health. Glad to get that straightened out." He watched her remove her clogs and skip swiftly down the stairs. A momentary sense of relief washed over his body, quickly replaced by an acute awareness that the potential for danger was far from over. He refocused, breathing purposefully, and reached inside his coat to pull out his .38 Smith & Wesson.

Lauren went down the two flights of stairs and stopped at the landing on the second floor. She had no desire to walk into a crime scene in the making, but she sure as hell wasn't going to abandon Sebastian altogether. She quickly put through the call to the police and waited for the sound of cars arriving below.

For the sound of gunfire from above.

Five minutes and four Our Fathers and five Hail Marys later—for a totally lapsed Catholic, it was amazing how the words tumbled out—the boys in blue arrived.

The shots didn't.

Lauren supposed she should be relieved. And she was—until she saw that Ricky Volpe was one of the beat cops.

"Laurie, you the one to call in a potential B and E?" Ricky asked. No "Are you all right?" No "You're not hurt, are you?" It figured. Back in high school it was well-known that Ricky's concept of foreplay was to unzip his pants.

"Yeah, good to see you, too, Ricky." She nodded toward her apartment. "My place is the next floor up. A colleague and I noticed the door was open. He's still up there, checking thing's out."

"Oh, yeah?" Ricky shook his head. "A regular Arnold Schwarzenegger?"

Lauren thought about the image for a moment. "Actually, more like Benicio del Toro."

"He's Hispanic?"

Lauren shook her head. "Never mind. In any case, he's the only one in my apartment wearing a three-thousand-dollar suit, unless whoever broke in has this thing for Armani, as well."

Ricky raised his eyebrows. "Armani, huh?" He unholstered his gun and faced his partner. "Let's see what gives, and try not to dirty the fancy tailoring at the same time."

What a wit. Lauren started to follow them up the stairs. Ricky swerved around. "You, half-pint. Stay put until I call you." He turned around and the two men headed up the stairs.

Half-pint! Lauren was disgusted. She waited for a count of ten, then followed on up. From the end of the hallway she could see that the door to her apartment was wide open. Sebastian was standing in the middle of her living room-slash-dining-room-slash-kitchen. He had his hands on his hips. His jacket was pushed back and his head was bent down as he talked to Ricky's partner. His face was set in a grim line. He periodically nodded his head toward various parts of the room.

Lauren walked to the doorway and stopped. What greeted her was a disaster area akin to the proverbial trailer park after a tornado.

Ricky came back from checking out her bedroom and bathroom and holstered his gun. "Holy cow, Laurie. This is one hell of a mess," he said, shaking his head. "You know, you're mother's going to freak when she hears about this."

Lauren gave him a steely gaze. "And who's going to tell her? If you so much as breathe a word about this, I will personally come and put tiny holes in all the packets of condoms in your medicine cabinet, or bed stand, or wherever you keep them. Then the neighborhood will really have something to talk about nine months from now."

"Hey, you're one to knock my social life," Ricky said defensively. "Anyone who goes out with Johnny Budworth shouldn't talk. Oh, that's right, he dumped you."

Lauren narrowed her eyes. "Just to set the record straight, I was the one who dumped him."

Sebastian cleared his throat. "Not to break up this cozy tête-à-tête," he drawled, "but I do believe we have a crime scene to investigate. I've already told Officer Greene here what I know." He nodded to the junior partner, who really did look wet behind the ears. His shoes were spit polished and his hair trimmed to within a millimeter of his pumpkin-shaped head. His biceps bulged in a way that spoke of a close working relationship with the weight room and dietary supplements.

Ricky spread his legs and hooked a thumb into a side pocket. "And you would be, exactly…?"

Lauren sighed, wondering how the situation had gone from being about her to about them. "Officer Ricky Volpe, this is Sebastian Alberti, an art theft investigator out of D.C."

Ricky and Sebastian suffered a nod at each other. It was only slightly more elevated than the way more lowly male species sniffed each other's rear ends.

"Ricky and I grew up together, graduating from Our Lady of Victory Grammar School," Lauren explained with a certain amount of disgust. "Luckily the gods intervened and we parted ways in high school when Ricky went to LaSalle Academy, a Catholic military school in South Philly—a combination that only the Jesuits could have dreamed up."

"Hey," Ricky said defensively. "I'll have you know that we won the parochial league basketball championship when I was captain my senior year."

"I'm sure it was the high point of your life," Sebastian said sardonically.

Ricky looked to say thank you, then realized maybe he should think better of it. He turned to Lauren. "You notice anything that's missing?"

Lauren did a quick survey. "In here, a boom box from the bookshelf. Maybe some CDs. Hey, a thief who likes Motown—there's a clue for you." Her eyes circled back to the table. "I won't know about the papers until I go through them, but I can tell you my laptop's missing—a PowerBook G5." That hurt. She'd just gotten it. She walked over to the kitchen counter and rifled through a wicker basket that served as a catchall for take-out menus, keys and loose change.

"Hey, don't touch anything. I'm gonna have some guys dust for prints," Ricky called out.

Lauren looked up, distracted. "Oh, sorry. I was just checking if I still had a backup to my work on the computer." She held up the small memory stick that fit into the USB port on her laptop—or what used to be her laptop. Then she took a few steps across what the real estate agent had euphemistically called the "galley kitchen" to the miniscule oven. She pulled down the door to the gas model and peered in.

"Hey, Laurie, kid, let's not do anything desperate." Ricky moved toward her uncertainly.

"Fear not, Ricky." Lauren stood up straight again. In her hand, she held a steno notebook. "I keep my files in the oven."

Sebastian angled his head. "You don't find that a little awkward when you cook?"

She blinked innocently. "Who cooks?"

Ricky made a face. "And to think you come from South Philly." He looked at his partner. "Get this down, will you?"

"About where she keeps her files?" Officer Greene stared vacantly.

Ricky frowned and addressed Lauren again. "Any previous break-ins, either at your place or in the building or neighborhood?"

She shook her head. "Not that I know of, but then I've only been here a few weeks." She distractedly pointed to the unopened boxes as evidence of her short time in the place.

"So you can't think of any reason why you were hit in particular?" Ricky asked.

Lauren shook her head. "It's not like I leave cash lying around or have anything valuable like jewelry. My high school ring is only twelve-carat gold."

"Well, on the surface of things, it all looks like your typical breaking and entering to me. You might want to get your landlord to invest in some decent locks." He waved his thumb toward the door. "A juvenile delinquent with half a brain could pick those."

Lauren caught a glimpse of Sebastian's frowning expression. "You think differently—that the locks are good enough?"

"No, I think even a Labrador retriever with no brain could pick those locks." He shook his head. "It's the motivation I question." He worked his jaw and added, "Maybe we're looking at a falling-out among thieves?"

Lauren rolled her eyes. She seemed to do a lot of that around Sebastian Alberti. "Oh, for the love of Mike. Will you give it a rest? I've just had my brand new apartment burgled and you're giving *me* a hard time? Ricky—" she looked pointedly at the cop "—don't even follow up on that line of questioning. I take back anything I may have said that seemed to compliment Mr. Alberti's investigative skills."

Sebastian shrugged.

Officer Greene slapped his pad shut. "The team should be here real soon to dust for prints, but truthfully, I'm not holding out much hope. Once you've gone through the place, you'll need to come down to the station to file a claim for what's missing. Meanwhile, maybe you should think about staying somewhere else for the night, or at least until you get the locks changed."

Lauren nodded. "Nothing like being driven out of my own house before I've had a chance to color coordinate my bathroom towels with my shower curtain."

"Sorry?" Officer Greene furrowed his concerned brow.

Lauren shook him off. "Never mind. I tend to use sarcasm in times of stress."

"Next you'll be spouting Shakespeare," Ricky said. "Then we'll really be in trouble."

"Is that your way of offering comfort?" Lauren gave him a withering look.

"Listen, kid, I'd give your insurance agent a call and chalk it up to bad luck," Ricky advised.

"Not to mention bad locks," Sebastian added.

Ricky tipped his head. "And that, too."

Lauren swallowed deliberately. "All right." She went to usher out the policemen but stopped a few feet short of the doorway. "Hey, Ricky, you wouldn't know anyone who works on the Camden force? In the Roebling area?"

"You think there's a connection?"

Lauren shook her head. "No, it's for a story I'm working on with my friend here."

Ricky worked his upper lip, then let his jaw drop open stiffly. "Remember Walt Mahoney?" Lauren frowned. "He was captain of Xavier's basketball team? The only school to whip our butts in the regular season?"

"Bunch of dirty players. But you're right."

Ricky nodded. "Mahoney works out of the precinct in that neighborhood." He walked to the door. "But, hey, you know that neighborhood's pretty rough. You want to watch yourself going over there."

"Don't worry. She won't be alone," Sebastian said.

Ricky eyed Sebastian and acknowledged his terse statement with a grunt as he left with his partner. Lauren would never understand male communication skills, or lack thereof.

She slowly closed the door. She breathed in deeply, straightened her shoulders and turned to face the inevitable. "Well, it's a good thing I'm not an acquisitive person. Otherwise trying to salvage this mess could be kind of upsetting." Who was she kidding? She was devastated, not so much by the material loss, but at the notion of being violated. She'd only had a glimpse through the doorway into her bedroom. Even then, she saw that the room had been tossed. Somehow, that bothered her more. She couldn't contain a shiver that ran the length of her body.

A shiver that Sebastian noted right away. He studied her resolute expression, and he could tell she was trying to put a good face on a bad—very bad—situation, but her anxiety was just as clearly evident. She was right: poker was not a professional alternative.

He fought down the unfamiliar urge to embrace her in his arms and offer comfort. After all, he was here to get to the bottom of a crime—not be her friend.

Which didn't explain at all then, why the next thing that came out of his mouth was, "When I said you wouldn't be alone, I meant it. You're moving in with me."

6

LAUREN'S HEAD SNAPPED UP. "What? What are you talking about?"

What *was* he talking about? The truth of the matter was that his impulsive statement was probably more a shock to *his* system than hers. Sebastian couldn't remember the last time he'd invited a woman to a hotel room.

In matters of sex, Sebastian had a strict policy regarding one-night stands with anonymous partners. N-O.

It was a matter of mathematics, really. As someone who dealt with crime, he was constantly assessing risky behavior. And casual sex with strangers was simply too risky. Far better for him to engage in intermittent interludes of passion with charming, intelligent women. Women who commanded his respect and stimulated his libido, and who made their careers a priority and thereby understood the rules of engagement. In other words, what they were entering into was shared mutual pleasure with no expectation of any personal attachment, long-term or otherwise.

As for his sudden invitation to Lauren Jeffries…it wasn't a question of sex. Well, maybe partly, but only partly. Sebastian was sufficiently self-aware to comprehend that his offer was a gesture of friendship.

And that was something totally new.

To put it bluntly, Sebastian didn't have friends. Yes, he had the admiration of his colleagues and socialized with them on occasion. He was also a favorite among Washington hostesses, who frequently sought him out as a witty and sophisticated dinner guest. But real friends—the kind you shared your hopes and dreams, your disappointments with—those he didn't have.

Why? Because he didn't need them, or so he always told himself. But with Lauren, his steely resolve to isolate himself was, well, less steely. Her vulnerability, which she tried fiercely to deny, was piercing his carefully constructed emotional chain mail. And in turn, he was ready to charge to her rescue, wear her standard and vanquish her foes.

Sebastian scowled. The physical threat to Lauren Jeffries was all too real. But that wasn't what was troubling him. After all, he'd found himself in danger before. No, it was the emotional threat to himself.

Sebastian knew that if he offered to help her, he was also exposing how he felt. He would face the risk of not being accepted or understood, of disappointing someone because he was not one thing or another. All of his instincts told him to pull back and remain outside the emotional fray.

There was something about Lauren though, something that went beyond her fragile beauty and her luscious body and dragged him into the world of true friendship, not to mention, emotional intimacy. He shuddered. Emotional intimacy. Next he would be quoting Freud.

Then he looked at her face—still startled from his unexpected invitation—and knew anything was possible.

Sebastian worked his lips. "I'm saying that once the police are through here, you should pack a bag with items you'll need for a few days and move into my hotel room with me."

"Don't be ridiculous. I mean, I can understand that it'd be totally stupid to stay here until the locks are changed, but in the meantime I can just call Phoebe. I'm sure she'd have no problem with me bunking with her for a while. Her place is large enough to hold all the starting players for the Sixers *and* a number of substitutes. For all I know, for that matter, she already has." She saw Sebastian slant her a curious glance, and shrugged her shoulders. It wasn't her job to explain her friend's—shall we say—all-embracing social life.

Sebastian came over and stood close—a little too close. "As much as that statement begs elaboration, and in some circles might offer real appeal for staying at her place, I don't think you want to jeopardize Phoebe."

"You think this break-in was more than what it appears?" His earlier statement about "a falling-out among thieves" was preposterous. But the notion that the crime hadn't been a random occurrence wasn't.

"You're saying is that whoever did this"—she nodded around the room "—is really after me?"

"For any number of reasons. And if you stay with me, not only will you be safe…" Sebastian lowered his chin and looked at her from under his slanted brows.

He stared into her face. Somehow, some way, Lauren Jeffries had managed to tap into his supremely suppressed capacity to trust. Trust that one individual would not mess with his psyche and leave it in broken shards.

He raised his hand and rubbed her baby-fine hair, the gesture releasing a sweet fragrance of innocence—or maybe just the remnants of her conditioner. Whatever. He smiled. To himself and at her. He placed his thumb on her forehead and gently rubbed away the furrowed lines of worry. "Trust me." *Just as I trust you*, he thought but didn't say.

"You think?" The corner of her mouth twitched up.

He breathed in slowly, studying the curved line that cupped the corner of her delectable mouth. "I know."

Then he bent his head and touched his mouth to those full pink lips of hers, lips that begged to be kissed. It was a feathery kiss that tasted of coffee and spoke of laughter, newness, promise.

And it had Lauren's heart thumping like the bass line of a Led Zeppelin track. She pulled back—not because she didn't like it, but because she knew she liked it—a lot. She noticed how dilated Sebastian's pupils had become. And even with the space between their bodies, she felt his heart pumping erratically.

"As invitations go, that's a whopper." She supposed she should have acted more coolly, but with her body temperature hovering close to tropical limits, cool was not possible. "Are you sure I'll be safe if I go back with you to your hotel?" The question wasn't just rhetorical.

She knew. He knew it, as well.

Sebastian shook his head. "Frankly, I'm not sure *I'll* be safe."

LAUREN SURVEYED THE irregularly shaped hotel suite, with its dormer windows and impeccably tasteful furniture, including an immense armoire holding enough electronic paraphernalia to launch the Sixth Fleet. She craned her neck toward the bathroom and caught a glimpse of the most enormous bathtub this side of the Delaware River.

The Rittenhouse, a boutique hotel on posh Rittenhouse Square, defined luxury at its most discreet. But since it was an independent, as opposed to one of the luxury chains, it didn't usually cater to high-flying business travelers.

"Somehow I would have pegged you for more the Ritz-Carlton type." Lauren referred to the opulent neoclassical hotel on Broad that looked like a vision of the Pantheon on steroids.

"If I want to be surrounded by white marble, I can go to the White House."

She watched him drop his keys on the side table by the door. Even Lauren, who was hardly a home furnishings guru, recognized the fine woodworking and curved lines of the Biedermeier piece. "Not bad accommodations," she volunteered.

Sebastian looked around with a more jaded eye. "Trust me, after a while, all hotel rooms look alike."

"Easy for someone to say who's used to spending over two hundred dollars a night," Lauren scoffed.

"Easy for someone to say who's used to spending over two hundred days a year in hotel rooms."

Lauren was incredulous. "Really?"

"Really."

Lauren blinked. It made sense that someone in his position had to travel, but to be that rootless? "Don't you get lonely?"

Sebastian shrugged. "It's not like there's anyone to miss."

Her heart immediately skipped a beat.

"Though I do miss…" He paused.

"You miss?" she prompted nervously.

He looked up without focusing on anything in particular. "I miss a sense of home and the security and peacefulness that comes with it."

"You mean D.C.?"

Sebastian glanced her way and laughed quietly. "No, I have a place in the country. When I'm there, I get to be a curmudgeonly hermit to my heart's content."

"But if you're all by yourself, aren't you still lonely?"

Sebastian thought a moment. "There can be contentment in being alone."

Lauren winced. "But don't you want more than contentment? Don't you ever yearn for warmth, companionship, laughter?"

It sounded so tempting, especially coming from Lauren Jeffries. Yet, the old demons were strong. "You know, my daddy used to say that sometimes we get what we deserve."

"Please, that sounds like something out of Dante or Tennessee Williams," she said with exasperation. "But, still, get real. Of course you deserve more…just look at you. You're handsome, sophisticated, successful."

Sebastian arched his eyebrows. "I like the sound of this."

Lauren was about to give him his comeuppance for that smarty-pants remark when she suddenly realized that although Sebastian Alberti might display the trappings of wealth, he never bragged about his position. If anything, he was tight-lipped, modest to a fault. Which immediately reminded her of something he'd said casually just a few minutes ago.

"You've been to the White House, haven't you? And I don't just mean to take the tour."

Sebastian shrugged. "Maybe once or twice. It was no big deal." True, he had managed to track down a Klimt, which had originally belonged to a member of the White House Counsel's family, and which the Nazis had illegally confiscated during the war. And then there was the other time when he had successfully completed a behind-the-scenes negotiation regarding disputed artworks in a traveling exhibit from the Kunsthistorisches Museum in Vienna.

These actions hadn't garnered any publicity. In fact, that was the whole point.

"'No big deal' you say," Lauren scoffed. "Why do I think there's a lot more to that simple statement than you're letting on?" She walked to the window. Talk about a million-dollar view.

"Contrary to your reporter's inclinations, darlin', sometimes a simple statement is just that—a simple statement."

Lauren raised an eyebrow and pivoted around to regard him. "I don't know. Somehow I don't think there's anything simple about you, Sebastian Alberti."

"And you, Lauren Jeffries? Is there anything simple about you?" Sebastian stepped toward her. The window was open and a light evening breeze billowed the sheer curtain at her feet. The lamp on the table cast a glow around her lithe body, making her seem ethereal—and oh, so very real at the same time.

Lauren watched him draw nearer, her own feet rigidly affixed to the Aubusson carpet. He reached for her hand. Her fingers trembled in his. In fear. In anticipation. "What do you mean?" she managed to ask as her gaze locked onto his sensual mouth.

He lightly brushed her cheek with the pad of his thumb. She shivered in response. "What I mean is, are you what you seem?" He rubbed back and forth.

Lauren nodded, her whole sensory system zeroing in on the touch of his skin on hers. "Yes, yes," she sputtered. "I'm exactly what I seem." She swallowed the hard-boiled egg-size lump in her throat. "Don't you believe me?"

He cupped her jaw and let his fingers trail down her slender neck. "I almost could." He angled his head this way and that. She looked so open, so vulnerable. His conscience kicked in, in response. "I'm not keeping you from work at the paper, am I?"

She shook her head. "Miraculously, today was a

slow news day. If you don't count you, that is." Not likely. "And the hydrant story I'll take care of with a few phone calls tomorrow and Monday."

How was he supposed to do the noble thing and not take advantage of her when she was making herself so available? Friends didn't exploit friends, he was pretty sure of that. But could he really categorize what he was feeling right now as friendship? He'd try. "You've just suffered a traumatic experience. Maybe you should just get some rest?"

Lauren felt a surge of disbelief. Was he suddenly rejecting her? Now that she had agreed to come back to his room because she couldn't stay at her place, but also because—my God—the guy was drop-dead gorgeous, not to mention brave, charming and had lips that could make more music than Louis Armstrong's trumpet? It wasn't possible.

It was time for her to step up to the plate. She put her small but extremely competent—and right now, extremely forceful—hand on his chin and turned his face to her. "So call me crazy, but I figure you want me to kiss you?"

Sebastian peered down at her hand. But he didn't move. If anything, he leaned farther into her grasp. "Kissing would be nice."

"Just nice?" She spread her hand over his cheek.

He smiled into her palm, and Lauren could feel the corner of his mouth press into her skin. "It depends on how it's done."

She brought her other hand up, at the same time rising on tiptoe. She wet her lips and tasted, tasted the full sweetness of his lower lip with a soft kiss, then a firmer bite. Firm enough to have him parting his mouth so that she could dip her tongue inside while her lips mated with his for a long, long sigh.

And when she was done, and the black spots were clearing from the back of her eyeballs, Lauren tentatively withdrew. Not that she wanted to pull away, mind you. What she really wanted was to rip away at that perfectly tailored suit of his, loosen his designer tie and spray the tiny white buttons of his dress shirt across a carpet whose net value exceeded her outstanding college loans by a factor of ten or so. "So how was that for 'done'?" she asked.

He caught one of her hands in his and brushed his lips across her knuckles. Lauren looked into his eyes, and believe it, care was the last thing she saw in his dilated pupils.

"I'd say that was done perfectly." He flipped her hand over and left a trail of small kisses along the inside of her wrist.

Lauren inhaled loudly. Now for stage two. "But not enough, right?"

Sebastian held himself still. "Are you sure you want to do this? You don't strike me as the kind of woman who just follows men to their hotel rooms. For that matter, I'm not the kind of man who invites women to his hotel room, either."

His admission moved her even more than his kiss, and that was saying something. Now she knew for sure that Sebastian didn't enter into things casually—and when he did, it was with all his heart. He so deserved more than mere contentment. And come to think of it, so did she.

For a woman who had had the guts to get out of

the neighborhood and prove herself professionally all on her own, Lauren had played it safe on the personal front. Okay, she'd had the good sense to break off her engagement, but where had she dared to tread since then? Nowhere. She'd ignored her feelings and guarded her emotions. Well, she knew that *now* was the time to spread her wings with a man who needed to find solid ground. Talk about an oxymoron come to life.

"Do I want to do this?" She repeated his earlier question. Was she really going to jump into bed with a man the first day she'd met him? With only a handsome face and a great body, the answer was an emphatic no. But with a man who had so much to give and deserved to receive just as much in return? You bet.

Lauren raised her eyes and answered frankly, "You and I both know it's more than a question of want." And then because she was brave, though nervous at the same time, she couldn't resist masking her acute emotions with a burst of sarcasm. "Let's just say the high-quality furnishings, idiosyncratic room configuration and high-speed DSL connection have turned me into a wanton sex slave."

Sebastian raised an eyebrow.

Her humor was a shock, until he comprehended that it was her safety mechanism. She was willing to take the plunge, willing to take the risk despite the circumstances. And her fearlessness made him disregard the obvious objections—that they'd only met, that they were working together, and that she was even possibly involved with the crime. Because she was right. This was more than a question of mere wanting. This was connecting in a way he had never dared.

Lauren slumped with impatience. "Oh, please, would you just jump my bones now—as in pronto? Otherwise, I'll be forced to find something else to do that can help slake all this pent-up sexual energy. I mean, do you really want to watch me unpack my bag and lay out my clothes in a regimentally neat fashion in one of the dresser drawers, only to be followed by me writing out a list of phone calls—in order of emotional importance in addition to area code—that I should make to people to let them know where to reach me in case of an emer—"

"Lauren?" Sebastian nuzzled the side of her neck before placing his mouth next to her ear.

"Yes?" she asked in a strangled voice as she let her head fall back.

He bit her lobe, and she couldn't have told you the metropolitan Philly area code if her life depended on it. "You can call later," he said as his hand snaked under the edge of her sweater and came into contact with her midriff. He ran his fingers across her ribs and eased them to the bottom of her silky bra.

Lauren grabbed his shoulders. "No problem. Only kiss me, would you? Let me know I'm doing the right thing?"

And he did. He started fiercely, but finished gently. "Do you know now?" he asked, and she leaned into him, giving her answer with the touch of her body. He ran his thumb along the curved top of her bra cup. His calluses lightly abraded her skin in a way that sent a snap, crackle and pop from her toe-nails on upward, only stopping in key, very key, spots. "How about you just relax?"

She gasped. "I don't think that's possible." She pulled her head back. "Though maybe if you kissed me again, it might work."

"Anything to oblige the lady." And he took her face in his hands and offered a kiss with so much fervor that had Lauren begging for more.

And he gave it. His other hand magically disap-peared under her sweater, as well. Even more magi-cally, her sweater disappeared—over her head with only a minor snag when the turtleneck caught on the tip of her nose.

Lauren stood there naked from the waist up, ex-cept for a beige bra that she had bought at thirty per-cent off at Kohl's. It wasn't the newest thing under the sun, and the elastic bits were getting that ruffled, tired look. "I realize my underwear isn't exactly the glam, seductive type, but I wasn't exactly anticipat-ing this little escapade when I dressed myself for work this morning. And I'm hopeless when it comes to washing my bras in those little mesh lingerie bags," she babbled.

"Well, if you're that unhappy, we'll just have to do something about it," Sebastian said. And with a dexterity that spoke highly of his motor skills and his personal knowledge of the ins and outs—though technically, more the offs—of lingerie, he swiftly unfastened her bra and tossed it over the back of the velvet-covered chair near the table. "There, you see? No need to worry about little mesh laundry bags." He let his eyes focus on her breasts for a long, drawn-out moment before raising his hands to her trousers. "What is a little mesh laundry bag anyway?"

Lauren gazed down and watched him undo the button at her waistband. "It seems you're the one doing all the work."

He stilled his fingers. "You have any objections?"

She actually gave his question some thought. "Strangely enough, no. It's really very liberating to let someone else take charge." She paused. "You realize that any minute now, I'm likely to be completely naked?"

"And what a pleasant realization that is." With one hand holding the loose waistband, Sebastian used the other to unzip her trousers. Then he slipped them over her hips.

I really must ease up on the ginger ales, Lauren thought immediately when the material didn't fall effortlessly to the floor the way it seemed it should. "Sorry. My hips are kind of large for my body—a tendency of all the Jeffries women, you see. I tried jogging, but that just seemed to make my calves bigger," she prattled self-consciously, looking across the room and wondering if the colorful print on the opposite wall was a genuine Chagall. Something about getting naked in front of an impossibly sexy man was bringing out insecurities that she thought she'd buried in her teenage years. The inner chubby girl seemed to be resurfacing.

She looked down and was startled to see Sebastian now kneeling in front of her. In pulling her pants down to her knees he had simultaneously taken down her underpants, something she hadn't noticed until this moment. "Gee, you're quick."

He grazed his lips over her hipbone and kissed it lightly. "If all the Jeffries women have hips like yours, you must be the fantasy of the whole male population of Philadelphia. And, darlin', while the pleasure is certainly mine to gaze on you this way, the idea is for you to have even more pleasure." He moved his face to her stomach and rubbed his mouth back and forth before breathing in the warmth of her skin. "So I hope this is not too quick."

"No, not too quick," she croaked as his mouth drifted southward toward wilder territory. She closed her eyes and leaned her head back.

"Sit," he said, and pooled her pants around her ankles.

She blinked her eyes open. "Sit?"

"Yes, in the chair behind you. I need to finish up here."

Lauren glanced down. She felt awkward about investigating too closely, which was really ridiculous because it was her body, after all. But, okay, her awkwardness was what it was, and she looked down. "Oh, right, my clogs. They're in the way." She reached back to grab the arm of the chair before sitting down. The velvet fabric felt soft against her bottom.

Sebastian quickly disposed of her shoes and socks, and the pants came sailing off with ease. At which point Lauren was acutely aware that she was completely naked and Sebastian had yet to remove a stitch of clothing, let alone undo his top button and loosen his tie. "Maybe it's your turn now?" she inquired about the obvious.

"Actually, I was thinking it's more yours." He

leaned forward and spread her thighs apart, and Lauren found herself doing mental math to figure out when she had last shaved her legs. He reached up with one hand and feathered the triangle of darker blond curls between her legs. She stopped worrying about shaving. He probed with his thumb and found the slit. Slowly, he inserted the edge of his finger and circled the entrance to her vagina. "I think it's time to finish things here," he said, and plunged his finger inside her.

Lauren just about rocketed off the chair. And just about died when she saw his head go in the direction of his exploring hand.

She'd been expecting to have sex, but not this. THIS. Guys in South Philly—at least the guys she knew—did not go down.

"Sebastian," Lauren gasped. His tongue followed the path that his fingers had taken. She could feel a rosy blush rise up her body. "This is velvet."

Sebastian flicked his tongue back and forth over Lauren's clitoris and she grabbed the arms of the chair to keep from sliding off. "This is more than velvet," he growled softly. "It's apricots and honey, it's sweet ambrosia." He sucked her sensitive bud into his mouth, at the same time thrusting more forcefully with his finger.

Lauren heard herself panting. "No, the chair. It's velvet. I don't want to—" And then she couldn't protest anymore because a contraction hit her body with a force that knocked the words from her lips, the thoughts from her brain.

So much so that it was in a kind of a drugged haze that she figured out that he was carrying her to the bed. Somehow the brocade cover and Austrian down duvet were stripped clear, and she was lying on cool, ironed sheets. Even more essentially, Sebastian was also stripped of his suit and tie and shirt and shoes and socks. It all happened so quickly that she didn't have a chance to see if he wore boxers or briefs.

"See, are you happy? No more velvet." He slid the naked length of his body next to hers.

Lauren stared. Well, who wouldn't? The man was downright gorgeous, muscular in all the right places, and flat and angular in the appropriate others. A light dusting of dark hair formed a triangle across his powerful chest, and Lauren reached out and touched it. She drew her fingers back and forth between his brown nipples. He hissed when her fingers abraded his skin. She must remember that for later, not now. Now she was too anxious to linger.

Instead, she let her hand travel down his stomach, following the narrowing line of his chest hair that led to the darker thatch at the top of his legs. And where his erection was standing proudly. She reached out and circled it. Heat radiated from the smooth skin. And with her fingers wrapped tightly around him, Lauren slowly worked her hand from the base to the tip. Her index finger toyed with the drop of liquid that pearled at the top.

Sebastian breathed in sharply.

"I'm not so sure about the velvet part," Lauren said coyly. She worked her hand up and down his rigid member.

Sebastian rolled over on top of her, his body

crushing hers, her hand still wedged between them. Not only was Lauren's hand touching him intimately, the back of it was pressed into her most sensitive area. He ground his hips into hers, and her hand worked its magic on both of them. She should have felt embarrassed. Instead she felt wanton, totally turned on. She brought her mouth to his and kissed him in a way that mimicked the ferocious interplay already occurring lower in their bodies. To say the effect was erogenous was like saying the Hoover Dam was a water stopper.

Sebastian tore his lips from hers. "I'm sorry, we'll go slower next time. Now, I can't take any more." He raised his chest from hers and reached over to the nightstand. Jerking open the drawer, he grabbed a condom. Then he sat up on his knees while Lauren panted and watched him roll the latex down the length of him, and while he watched her watch him.

Then he was back on top, his hand moving between her legs. She opened wide when she felt the tip tease the entry to her body. He slowly eased farther, and pulled out, only to move farther in again. It was good, so good she thought she would die.

But she didn't. Instead she found herself dying for more. She shook her head and placed her hand on his back. "I want you deeper." She wrapped her legs around the backs of his thighs and raised her hips. "Deeper."

And he gave her more. Cradling her hips with one arm, he raised her off the bed and plunged to his full length. Harder, faster, he rode her, their bodies coated with a light sheen, their breaths coming in ragged gasps.

Lauren felt the tremors build deep within. She had climaxed on the chair, but now she felt like she was coming apart, coming undone. She went to hold back from the force, but he wouldn't let her. He dipped his head and, sucking on a nipple, drove toward the very core of her being.

And then there wasn't any core, just a phenomenal shattering of matter and nerves and emotions that ripped a stunned outburst from her lips, to be followed by an even louder one from his.

Afterward, they lay limply in each other's arms, breathing—barely breathing—until Sebastian stumbled to the bathroom, leaving Lauren momentarily to herself. As the exhaustion slowly crept from her body, the realization of what they'd just done replaced it. Which made Lauren wonder, *wonder if it was possible for your life to alter just like that?* Because just like that, her life seemed to have changed in some fundamental way.

Whether that was good or bad, she wasn't sure. Yes, the sex had been good—truly, madly, fabulously good—but the aftermath? Was she supposed to just go on coolly working with—let alone sleeping with—this guy who had trouble believing she wasn't out to double-cross him? She pulled the sheet up defensively and covered her body. Maybe it would be better if she reconsidered the wisdom of staying in his hotel room and braving the new experience of opening her heart to him?

But then Sebastian walked back in the room, and with his eyes on her, moved toward the bed—only to trip over her small duffel bag in his path.

"Ow." He hopped on one foot and stumbled onto

the mattress. "So much for my manly entrance." He brought his arms around her, turning her back into his stomach, and snuggled close. He rubbed the side of his face against her hair and kissed the top of her head. "You need anything?" he murmured, cuddling closer.

A man who knew how to snuggle was also a rare commodity in her neighborhood. Lauren felt his penis stiffen as it wedged against one cheek of her bottom. This was going beyond cuddling. She wiggled around and faced him. "How's your toe?" Maybe it *was* time to explore outside the neighborhood?

He frowned. "It hurts, but I'll live—live to fight another day."

She placed her hand on his chest. "Actually, I was thinking about other things besides fighting." Her fingers found one of his nipples and she scraped her nails across its puckered surface. Now she was good and ready to linger.

SEBASTIAN WOKE WITH A start, sensing he had missed something—in addition to his dinner. He turned his head to the side, and as soon as he did, he caught a whiff of something intoxicating. He smiled at the memory of making love to Lauren—the first feverish time when they'd gone at each other like hormonally driven teens; the second, when they'd lavished careful attention on each other. Yes, sirree. Sebastian wet his lips when he thought about the comprehensive attention Lauren had lavished on a particularly sensitive area. Talk about sublimely intoxicating. He would have almost called it a divine experience, except his body was still humming in a way that could only be described as carnal.

And speaking of carnal— He turned to the center of the bed and reached out with his arm, only to find a rumpled sheet and an indented pillow.

He looked around. The sun had long since set, and the light from outside street lamps slanted shadows across the already darkened room. But at the writing desk, he spied the glow of a computer screen. Hunched over in front of it, with one of the hotel robes seductively sliding off one shoulder, was the object of his current affection.

Was *affection* the right word? Certainly it was a word he'd never associated with himself before. Sebastian shrugged. He preferred to think of the term "current," and her soft, pliable body sitting within easy reach. He pulled back the covers and strode over, oblivious to his nakedness.

"Hard at work?" he asked, stopping to peer over her shoulder. He could see that Lauren had called up an art history search engine and was looking at paintings by Caravaggio.

"Hmm?" Lauren scrolled down the page and jotted some notes on a steno pad.

He propped his naked hip on the corner of the desk. "Expanding your knowledge of Italian art?"

She rubbed the side of her temple without looking over. "Just trying to find out what the stolen items look like. Your commission's site didn't post any photos, but since the artists produced other stuff, I thought I'd try to get a feel, put the pieces in some kind of context." She made some more notes on the Caravaggio works before tapping in Nicola

Pisano's name. Bent on her task, she seemed oblivious to Sebastian's presence.

Which frankly, yes, somewhat insulted his ego. Even though he assured himself his ego—as well as everything else—was quite nicely intact. In fact, something other than latent insecurity was starting to dance around in his brain. "And you just happened to remember the names of the artists in question?"

"I remember lots of things." Lauren didn't seem aware of his discomfort. "Jeez." She whistled. "Will you look at that marble altarpiece! What my parents' church wouldn't give for that beauty. Of course, they had trouble just raising enough money to fix the roof over the rectory last year."

"You were saying that you remember a lot of things?" Sebastian crossed his arms and leaned closer to the computer screen.

Lauren couldn't help but notice. She glanced up, finding herself within easy examining distance of the dark hairs on his muscled forearms. Her mind immediately brought into focus the picture of him holding her hips as he lowered his body to sink into her. She shook her head. "What's that?"

"I was wondering how you remember a lot of things, especially things like artists? Not your usual beat, as you informed me."

Lauren averted her eyes from his arms and tried to focus on something neutral. She landed on his chest—his very unclothed chest. No, no, that was definitely not something neutral.

She swung her eyes back to the screen. "It's an old memory trick I learned as a student. I go through the alphabet, and when I hit a certain letter that is the first letter in a name, it triggers the rest of it. Sometimes it doesn't have to be a letter. It can even be a sound-alike word that signals the name I'm looking for. I know it sounds kind of lame, but you can't believe how helpful it can be at times—and not just for things like press conferences. I mean, it's really kept me on Donna's good side, which—let me tell you—is no mean feat."

Sebastian narrowed his eyes. "Donna?"

"You remember. The elevator? The majordomo of the supply closet? The president of the Engelbert Humperdinck Fan Club?"

Sebastian nodded slowly. "Oh, that Donna."

"When the need arises, I can even mention favorite songs of his."

"You have favorites?" Sebastian appeared even more dubious.

"Well, not *my* favorite songs, but songs that are considered Engelbert Humperdinck's favorites, you know, hits. Here, I'll show you." She closed her eyes and started to recite the alphabet. "*A*—'After the Lovin', *B, C*," she mumbled. "Okay, *L*—'The Last Waltz'—"

Sebastian put his hand on her shoulder—the one that the robe had conveniently left bare. "It's fine. I believe you."

Lauren contemplated his hand. "Do you? And I don't mean about Engelbert's oeuvre. About me? And the art?"

Sebastian rubbed her shoulder blade with just the right amount of pressure. "If I believe anyone, I believe you."

Lauren wet her lips. "Okay, that's probably the best I can ask for at this point. But tell me, as long as we're sharing our professional secrets, why are you so keen to track down stuff like this?" She waved her hand at the photos of the priceless art on the computer.

"Because it's my job."

Lauren shook her head. "Not buying that. No one is that intense about his work just because it's a job. It has to be a passion. I mean, why would I wake up after the best sex of my life—" whoops, that just slipped out and Lauren hoped it passed beneath Sebastian's radar screen, but somehow she didn't think anything passed beneath his radar screen "—to look at art pictures. Because tracking down the story, digging out the truth is my passion. So what's yours? Is it solving the mystery? Wanting to right a wrong? I mean, really, what makes Sebastian run? Really?"

His hand stopped.

"Please, don't keep from rubbing just because you're deep in thought," she added.

Sebastian smiled and squeezed playfully. "That's what I like about you—focused on the essentials." He bent down and planted a light kiss on her shoulder blade. Then he sat up. "You want to know the answer, really? I guess it's a desire to return the works to their rightful places." He placed the tip of his tongue behind his top teeth. "No, it's more than that. It's about finding a true home. Art goes to the soul of people's identities. It's more than a commodity. It provides an emotional, intangible anchor—a sense of belonging, a cultural touchstone. Does that make any sense?"

As he spoke, Lauren couldn't help but notice that his kneading had become more insistent. There it was again—that theme of "home." She had obviously struck a chord, but she had the good sense to refrain from emitting a jubilant "Aha!" Because deep down, she had the feeling that Sebastian Alberti was far more comfortable about baring his body than baring his soul. Though, in making love this evening, Sebastian *had* bared some of his soul whether he had been aware of it or not. The actual verbalization would come eventually, with her patience and with his trust. And she would gain the latter, she knew, by revealing more about herself.

Meanwhile, speaking of bodies, she slanted her head and enjoyed a very nice eyeful. And this time she didn't bother to search for something neutral to focus on when she spoke. "Do I know what you mean about a sense of belonging?" Her eyes drifted from PG- to R- and on to X-rated zones. "I don't know, sometimes when I think of my family and the neighborhood, I kind of wish I didn't have so strong a sense of belonging. But not to change the subject—but to change the subject—there's something else I should do before I forget." She scooted around in the chair and placed a hand on his thigh. The skin was warm, the muscles hard. It would be hard to forget.

"You need to call the cop who works in Camden?" He observed her hand.

"Yeah, I need to do that, but that wasn't what I had in mind at the moment." She made a slow circle on his skin with her index finger.

"You need to call room service for something to

eat? I realize we missed dinner." Sometimes his gallantry astounded him.

"No, I'm fine."

Sebastian tweaked a smile. "I should have
known food wasn't on your mind. After all, you're
the woman who keeps her files in her oven."

"Hey, don't knock my filing system. It thwarted
a thief this afternoon. Don't forget, that's where I
found my notes on the real Harry Nord."

Sebastian recalled the ransacked apartment. "I'm
still remembering." He searched her face to see if
she was *still* upset.

"Well, forget remembering—with or without the
aid of the alphabet and sound-alikes. I have other
things in mind." She tugged at one of his hands and
rose.

Sebastian slipped off the desk and draped an arm
around her shoulders. "Is that so?"

"You bet. I think it's about time you introduced
me to the wonders of the Rittenhouse's high-end
plumbing—and I don't mean the bidet."

Sebastian lowered his hands and undid the knot
at the front of her robe. He watched as she let the
terry cloth garment ease off her arms and puddle on
the floor. "Darlin', for you I'm willing to manip-
ulate every spigot, every hose and every faucet in
any number of pleasing ways. And if you think of
any way that I've missed, I'm more than ready to be
open-minded."

7

LAUREN HUNG UP THE PHONE and pressed her fingertips to her temples.

"Another brouhaha down at the school board?" Phoebe asked. She was propped up against Lauren's desk. The straight skirt of her suit fit snugly but perfectly over her narrow hips, and the material was some tweedy mixture of lime green, pink and cream, with gold thrown in for good measure. In theory, it should have looked like the remains of a ticker tape parade. In practice, it looked great. Go figure.

"If only it *were* the school board." Lauren stared at the phone and wondered what shoe would drop next. "Seems there's a three-alarmer at Broad and Master in North Philly."

Phoebe rested her palms on either side of her hips for support. "Don't tell me someone torched the Freedom Theatre?" Phoebe looked horrified at the thought of the country's largest African-American playhouse going up in flames.

"Luckily, no. A warehouse a few buildings down. Still, there were people inside, so I can't just do a call-in." Lauren pulled out a desk drawer to grab another of her steno pads and a minitape recorder. After all her years in Metro she had become inured to most of the stupid and craven things people did to each other. But not fires. The sight of a burn victim was something she could not easily forget.

She stretched her hand toward the mug that held her stash of pens, twisted her hair up and stuck in a ballpoint pen to keep it all out of her eyes. Then she glanced down at her calendar to check that she wasn't going to miss any meetings while she was out in the field. Miraculously, there was nothing urgent other than her four o'clock in Camden to meet a fence—not the chain-link variety, either.

The call to Walt Mahoney, the former pride of Xavier's basketball team and Ricky's suggestion for whom to contact regarding the scumbags of Camden, had struck pay dirt. Well, maybe.

"Listen, Laurie," he'd said on the phone between bites of a soft pretzel, "if you're looking for offloaded art, the most likely source is Slick Frankie. Usually he deals more in silver and jewelry, but from time to time he's been known to trade in stuff like paintings—paintings not necessarily coming through the normal channels, which does not endear him to the art establishment. To put it another way, the Philadelphia Museum of Art does not regularly invite him to their black-tie gala."

"So how do I contact him?" Lauren had asked, barely able to contain her enthusiasm.

"Frankie lurks, but you might be able to get him on his cell phone." Walt rattled off the number.

Lauren copied it into her notebook. "Thanks, I owe you one."

There was a pause on the other end of the line. "Hey, I hear from Ricky that you and what's-his-name are no longer an item."

Lauren shook her head. "And did Ricky also mention my place had been burglarized, too?"

"Yeah, he said something about it."

Great, pretty soon the whole of her old neighborhood would know, including her mother and father. "Walt, it's been great talking to you, but I'm on deadline here, so I gotta run."

She'd hung up and looked at her watch before calling her mother to preempt any gossip. No big deal. This time of day, her mother was undoubtedly at the family's dry cleaning business, doing the books. So as casually as possible, Lauren left a message that since the locks were being changed in her building, she was temporarily staying with a visiting colleague at the Rittenhouse. No need to mention the colleague was a man.

Instead she'd recited the phone number and hung up. Next she dialed Slick Frankie the Fence. What a ridiculous name. He suggested meeting at the Camden Aquarium by the shark tank at four. "I find them relaxing," he'd whispered and abruptly broken the connection. Sure, whatever.

Right now, Lauren had a fire to cover. She opened the drawer and pulled her wallet out of her bag. She had just enough money for a taxi up there and could probably thumb a lift back from another reporter. She looked up. "I don't suppose you'd let me borrow your car for a few hours?"

Phoebe's vintage Jaguar was a thing to behold, and about as reliable as a twenty-year-old gigolo.

The thing practically required a full-time mechanic. And Phoebe *had* a full-time mechanic.

Lauren shook her head. "Never mind. Forget I even asked." She stuffed the bills back into her wallet and jammed her notebook and pens in her bag.

Phoebe watched critically. "Why not let Mr. Tall, Dark and Handsome drive?"

Lauren glanced up. "That's right. Tall, Dark and Handsome. I almost forgot." She reached for the small pad next to the phone and hurriedly scribbled a note to Sebastian, giving her whereabouts and a rough idea when she should be back in the office. That would give them plenty of time, she relayed, to make the four o'clock appointment over at Camden Aquarium with Slick Frankie, and either before or after, check out 38 Roebling, the address of the burglary reported by Bernard Lord. Lauren knew it would be too much to ask that Bernard lived there currently or even recently—reporting was rarely that easy—but maybe there'd be a neighbor who remembered him.

When she was just about finished, she looked over at Phoebe. "Thanks for reminding me. How could I have forgotten?" She looked into space. "Really, how *could* I have forgotten?" Lauren's voice had the dreamy quality of an ingénue in a Rodgers and Hammerstein musical—an ingénue after she'd just gotten laid, or was dreaming about getting laid. No, come to think of it, Rogers and Hammerstein was not the right metaphor.

"Aha!" Phoebe's snap comment cut short Lauren's reverie. "So the truth comes out about Mr. Tall, Dark and Handsome. I'm proud of you, girl, truly

I am. I must say, I had my suspicions last night when I called you and there wasn't any answer." Phoebe pursed her lips and waited. "So? Spill the whole thing."

"Actually, the reason I wasn't home was that I had a break-in."

"Ohmigod!" Phoebe jumped off the desk. "You weren't hurt were you?"

"No, of course not. It happened before I got home." Lauren finished signing her name on the note, then looked around, wondering where she should put it so that it would catch Sebastian's eye when he returned. For the past two hours he'd been on a conference call to Zurich—or was it Zagreb?— regarding another case. One thing was for sure, she didn't want him to think she had skipped out on him in an effort to hide any wrongdoing. "Anyhow, while the locks are being changed I'm staying at the Rittenhouse."

"You're staying at the Rittenhouse? Very nice, but you realize you're going to max out your credit card in a matter of days."

"Actually, it's not my credit card that's going to get hit with the damage." Lauren grabbed a push-pin from the bulletin board over her blotter. "Excuse me." She circled around Phoebe and tacked the note to the outside wall of her cubicle.

"Hey, you're not escaping without details," Phoebe called after her.

Lauren came back to her desk and slipped her brown tweed blazer off the back of her chair. "You want details? Well, the towels are very nice and fluffy and the soap is French-milled."

"You can tell me about the bathroom accoutrements another time. I want the skinny—all of it."

Lauren pushed an arm through a sleeve and shrugged on the jacket. "What is there to tell? I used the high-speed Internet connection. We ordered room service." She paused. "The earth moved—several times." She stashed all the stuff she needed into her bag.

Phoebe rubbed her hands together. "Give me more. I need to see the whole picture, hear some quotes. What kind of reporter are you anyway?"

"A working reporter who has to cover a story even as we speak." Lauren grabbed her bag. She really did have to go, but… She frowned and regarded Phoebe. "What would you say about someone who talks about finding peace at his place in the country and who is driven to restore things to their rightful homes?"

"I'd say he's either fixated with his mother—the whole hearth-and-home thing—or has watched too many episodes of *This Old House* on Public Television."

Lauren pondered Phoebe's answer. "I think the latter would be easier to deal with. In the meantime it's a three-alarmer for me before heading out to track down a lead on my Harry Nord obit." She saluted. "*Hasta la vista*, baby."

Lauren took a step forward and found Phoebe blocking her path. "Uh, Phoebe, dearest, you make a better door than window."

Phoebe held up her hand, undeterred. "This is for your own good. You have just informed me that you're following a lead on an obit you fabricated about a dead man?"

Lauren shook her head. "No, I'm following a lead on a man—possibly dead, though that's not for sure—who did exist, but who I didn't know about, but who seems to fit my fake obit."

Phoebe leaned forward. "Breathe out through your mouth in my direction. I want to double-check you haven't been drinking. You remember what happened that time you had three sambucas."

Lauren rolled her eyes. "Please, that was two years ago, when I hadn't completely gotten over the flu and hadn't eaten anything for almost four days. Given that scenario, *you* would have seen a marching band of Venusians outside Le Bar Lyonnaise, too." She pushed past Phoebe—only to smack into her nemesis, Huey.

Huey jumped away, leaving a trail of dandruff in his wake. "Sorry, I've got a cold, and I was looking for some Kleenex." He sneezed, dislodging little bits of sputum onto the wall of her office. Charming.

Lauren marched back to her desk and returned with a box of tissues. "Here, take this and don't even think about giving it back."

Huey mumbled thanks and shuffled away in a haze of Vicks VapoRub.

Phoebe gagged. "It really creeps me out, how that little troll has a way of sneaking up on a person. Do you think he was purposely lurking there, listening to our conversation?"

"Huey?" Lauren snorted. "He wouldn't know how to listen if his life depended on it, and even if he did, he'd get half the information wrong anyway. No, he was probably just stalking you after getting a load of how short your skirt is."

"Yuck, I don't know what's worse. Huey eavesdropping or stalking." Phoebe looked at her skirt. "It is nice, isn't it? An advance sample from the new St. John's line. I haven't worn a skirt this short since I played forward on the Baldwin varsity field hockey team. Did I tell you I was the highest scorer my senior year?"

"Somehow I think you did." Lauren performed another manic last-minute check of her bag and started to leave—yet again. "This time I really am out of here."

"All right. But don't forget about the soirée at the Vesper Boat Club tonight. You remember? I left the invitation on your desk last week." Phoebe followed her down the hallway as Lauren headed for the elevators. "You can bring along you-know-who, if you want. Unless you'll be tied up, that is." Phoebe waggled her carefully waxed brows. "I can see it now—you tied up, or maybe him?"

Lauren rolled her eyes and punched the Down button. "Please, the only tying up tonight will be the string around the pot roast at my parents'. In a moment of weakness I agreed to attend Friday family dinner." The elevator door opened and Lauren stepped in. She turned to face Phoebe. "But I tell you what, I'll try to pop into the Vesper gig late-ish. It'll be a good excuse to escape the usual nagging about why aren't I not married to a nice boy from the neighborhood and when am I going to stop hanging around such lowlifes."

"Then they haven't met Mr. You-Know-Who." Phoebe waved. "Toodle-oo."

"And it'll be over my toodle-oo-dead-body that

they do," Lauren announced through the closing metal doors.

So why did Lauren have a sinking feeling that another "yeah, right" was about to rear its ugly head?

IT WAS WORSE THAN SHE'D expected. A family had been squatting in the building, and three of the six members had perished before firefighters could reach them. One of the victims was a six-month-old child.

So despite the sunny skies and sixty-degree weather that normally would have been a godsend in April, Lauren felt herself shivering.

She thanked the fire inspector on the scene for his quote and slowly shut her notebook. Mindful of the maze of fire hoses, she stepped away from the site and blindly rummaged through her bag for loose change. She found everything else—sugarless gum wrappers, pen caps, tampons—but no coins.

She heard footsteps behind her and figured it was her fellow reporter from the *Inquirer*. She brushed her hair out of her eyes and continued to peer into her bag. "You wouldn't have forty cents, would you?" She pulled her head up.

And felt a shiver ripple down her body—a shiver that was only partly due to her lowered body temperature.

Sebastian eyed her critically. "From the looks of your blue lips, a couple of quarters isn't going to cut it. You need a cup of coffee."

Lauren blinked, the realization that he was standing next to her amidst the confusion and the mess only gradually sinking in. "It's nothing, really, honest," she stammered. Somehow the sight of his scowling face and impeccable charcoal-gray suit was bringing tears to her eyes. She brushed them away with the back of her hand. "My lips always turn blue when my feet get wet."

Sebastian expelled a gust of air in a sign of frustration. "Please, we both know you couldn't lie your way out of a paper bag. I talked to one of the firefighters. I heard about the kid. I know why you're upset. Why don't we get out of here and go someplace quiet?"

Lauren ran her hand through her hair. How easy it would be to let Sebastian take over, whisk her away into the tidy cocoon of his hotel room and make all the ugliness vanish. Only the world didn't work that way. Not for Lauren anyway.

Sebastian Alberti might think he was doing her a favor, but she knew that the good times with him weren't meant to last. As soon as they broke open the Harry Nord/Bernard Lord story and found what was or was not going to be found, he'd hightail it back to D.C. with a "thank you very much, it's been memorable," and she'd be stuck with a career that was hanging on by the barest of threads and a heart that she was increasingly worried might be left in tatters.

That was the problem with great sex—combined with mystery, manners and a certain guy's self-protective instinct to keep his psyche from being exposed—it tended to blind a gal to reality and make her want to grab on with all her might and make it all better. Talk about a fairy tale.

Let me tell you, South Philly was not built on

fairy tales. Maybe a couple of good rock 'n' rollers, but no fairy tales.

So she refastened her blowing hair with a pen and eked out a smile. "The offer's mighty tempting, but I really need to get back to the paper to file the story. Make deadline before heading out again to the Camden Aquarium. It's my job. It's what I do."

Sebastian scrutinized her expression. "You don't need to tell me about your work ethic. Though why you feel you need to give blood—literally, it sometimes seems—to that two-bit rag is beyond me."

"It's funny, but when the call came from the *New York Times* I sat there weighing my options." Lauren raised both hands, palms up, pretending to compare the fictitious job offer. "*New York Times* or *Philadelphia Sentinel*? You know, it wasn't even close. 'Sorry, Mr. Salzburger,' I said, 'but how can I leave the glamour and prestige of my hometown tabloid?'"

Sebastian grabbed her gruffly by her jacket sleeve and ushered her over to his car.

Lauren stared at the Mercedes. "Amazing. The cops cordon off the area, and you still manage to park nearby."

He unlocked the doors and practically shoved her in. Then he circled the car and put his keys in the ignition. Only he didn't turn on the engine.

Instead he banged his hands on the tooled leather steering wheel and slanted her a withering glance. "What is it about you? You make jokes when you should be tearing your hair out?"

"Coping skills, I guess?" She batted her eyelashes innocently.

"Denial is more like it. You're so intent on proving how tough you are, you refuse help when you need it. If it's so damn important that you file the story, you can use my laptop." He nodded toward the trunk of the car. "It's got Wi-Fi, so you can e-mail it back to the newspaper without a hitch. But you'll do it from somewhere where you can get a decent cup of coffee with a lot of sugar in it, and where you're not hassled by a managing editor with ill-fitting pants, who calls you 'little woman' when you clearly could run rings around him—even on one of your bad days. All right?" He inhaled dramatically.

Lauren pursed her lips and waited a beat. "I think I'm supposed to be flattered—despite the fact that you are yelling at me."

Sebastian rolled his eyes. "Do we have a deal?" At least his voice had moderated.

She bit her lip. "All right." When Sebastian started the engine, she covered her mouth with her hand and hid her smile. Gee, he had actually complimented her. "But you should know—I don't take sugar in my coffee."

Sebastian turned and narrowed his eyes.

Lauren held up her hands. "Okay. I'll take sugar. But just this once."

LAUREN STARED AT the gray bodies darting nervously back and forth. Turning to Sebastian, she pointed at the thick glass. "How come they never think of trying to get out?"

The two of them were standing in the dark interior of the Camden Aquarium. It would have been spooky except for the fact that droves of school children were crowding the exhibits and shrieking at the tops of their lungs. You'd think they'd never seen a shark before, let alone less exciting things like shad and scrod.

Lauren stared at the large tank of gray and white predators. They were neurotically swimming this way and that, displaying more energy than a bunch of four-year-olds with ADD *and* on a sugar high. And they had very white and very pointy teeth. They bore a strong resemblance to the land variety of sharks that Lauren came in contact with on a regular basis.

Sebastian glanced over his shoulder toward the tank. "If you lived in New Jersey, would you try to get out?"

Lauren nodded. "Good point." He seemed to be making any number of good points, she realized. After the fire, he'd taken her to Chink's, absolutely the best diner in North Philly, where she'd had a coffee—with two sugars. She'd cranked out the story in record time, only pausing once, when the impact of the tragedy hit. And then, wouldn't you know it, he'd ordered her the perfect pick-me-up—a chocolate egg cream. Amazing stuff those egg creams.

But his true stroke of genius occurred when she'd offered to pay and he'd said, "Don't be ridiculous. I'll give Ray the bill and insist that the paper reimburse me."

And now, at the aquarium, Lauren was still grinning. She answered as she watched his reflection in the glass, "Did I ever tell you that I like your style, Sebastian Alberti?"

Sebastian cocked an eyebrow. "You did. Several times, as I recall."

A self-satisfied reply if ever Lauren had heard one. "You know, a swelled hea—"

"Lauren Jeffries?"

The inquiry came from over Lauren's right shoulder. And the male figure who did the asking was carefully positioned in the murky hallway, making it difficult to get a good look.

"Yes?" She swiveled in the direction of the voice.

"No, don't turn around. Just keep looking at the fish while I tell you what's what. After you called, I checked out your story with Walt Mahoney, and he said you were kosher. And seeing as I owe Walt a favor, I decided to come after all. So tell me, I hear you're interested in information?"

Sebastian didn't bother pretending to regard the fish. He angled his head and shifted his feet. Lauren did likewise. "We're both interested in information," he said.

Slick Frankie lifted his chin. "Who are you? You don't look like a reporter. I'd say you're a cop, but your suit's definitely beyond the salary of a municipal employee. Of course, there's also the possibility that you're a cop on the take."

Sebastian shrugged off the insult. "Just call me an art lover."

"A very successful art lover," Lauren added.

Slick Frankie did a back-and-forth look between the two of them. "You work as a team?"

"Yes," said Lauren.

"No," said Sebastian.

They looked at each other. Slick Frankie rolled his eyes.

"Well, sort of," conceded Lauren.

"In this instance," Sebastian qualified. He cleared his throat. "The point is, we're interested in finding particular pieces of art."

"Do I look like the kind of guy who knows anything about art?" Slick Frankie stepped out of the shadows to reveal himself more fully. A middle-aged man of medium height, he had thinning hair and a comb-over. His khakis were loose-fitting. A Kiwanis Club emblem was printed on his nylon jacket. A pair of cream-colored New Balance walking shoes completed the outfit.

He definitely did not look slick. In fact, Lauren thought he could easily fit the part of the retiree flipping burgers at the neighborhood block party. Maybe that was why he was so good at fencing goods in back alleys.

Sebastian slipped his hand into his suit jacket—Slick Frankie flinched momentarily, displaying highly sensitive reactions for a member of Kiwanis—and pulled out a photo. It was the same one Sebastian had shown Lauren the day before.

"Specifically, we're interested in art connected with this man," he said. "Ever recall seeing him, possibly as much as ten to fifteen years ago? He would have been significantly older than what's shown here."

Slick Frankie barely glanced at the photo. "That's a long time ago to remember."

Sebastian held the picture out farther. "Look again. Jog your memory. And let's say I would appreciate it in a big way, a really big way. *Capisce?*"

Slick Frankie studied Sebastian before he switched his attention to the snapshot. "*Capisce.*"

Lauren nudged Sebastian. "The *Sentinel* doesn't pay sources," she whispered.

"It's nice to know it has some moral standards. Luckily, I don't work for the *Sentinel*."

"Flyboy, huh?" Slick Frankie asked.

"Navigator, World War II. He was shot down over Italy." Sebastian paused and studied Slick Frankie carefully. "Takes one to know one, am I right?"

Slick Frankie nodded. "Choppers, in Nam." He surveyed Sebastian critically. "You're more, what, Bosnia?"

Sebastian didn't blink. "Desert Storm."

Frankie shook his head. "Never did like the desert."

Lauren frowned at Sebastian. "You never told me you were in the military?" Something else he was keeping close to the vest.

"I'm not big on swapping war stories. We're here to track down some art, missing art. So tell me, does the picture ring a bell?" He waved the photo in front of Slick Frankie's nose one more time.

"There a name to go with the picture?" Slick Frankie asked.

"Lord. Bernard Lord," Lauren answered. She reached down into her bag, ostensibly to get a tissue, but at the same time turned on her mini-tape recorder.

Slick Frankie studied the photo a moment longer. "Maybe he's familiar, maybe he's not. He's a local, did you say?"

"We didn't. But he *was* born in Camden, lived in Philly, or across the river in Jersey," Lauren supplied.

"So what's our native son supposed to have had in his possession that interests you so much?"

"Several works," Sebastian answered. "A minor Caravaggio—"

"If there's such a thing as a minor Caravaggio, this I need to know," Slick Frankie commented.

"In addition, a Carolingian silver chalice and a pair of marble candlesticks attributed to Nicola Pisano," Sebastian finished up.

Slick Frankie whistled. "Quite a haul." He was silent for a moment. "Did he liberate them during his service for Uncle Sam?"

Sebastian shook his head. "Later, apparently, more like fifteen years ago."

"Now I get it. When I might have—and I say *might have*—come in contact with him." He glanced around as some schoolchildren rushed past. "Kids—you gotta love 'em. Hey, you—" he pointed his finger "—no running with pens like that." He smiled and returned his attention to the interview. "Now where were we?"

"You were about to tell us about encountering Bernard Lord roughly fifteen years ago?" Lauren steered the conversation back on track.

Slick Frankie studied Lauren carefully. "Local girl makes good, right?"

Lauren shook off his comment. "I don't really think that has anything to do with the conversation, but, yeah, I'm from Philly."

"Nice. I like to see young people stay close to their roots. My younger son, first thing you know, he moves to Tucson. Tucson! Who lives in Tucson?"

Lauren sighed. Loudly. "Arizonans. To get back to Bernard Lord—"

"Yeah, yeah, yeah," Slick Frankie said, acting as if he were going in that direction all along. "Hypothetically speaking, mind you, I would have to say that it's not easy unloading goods like the ones you mentioned. It takes a certain clientele—people who don't necessarily consider little things like documented provenance. In their case, the value might not even be what's important." He stared at Lauren while he spoke, choosing his words carefully.

"And do you know such people personally?" Sebastian asked.

Slick Frankie smiled. "Don't we all?"

"Can you be more specific? Can you link anyone with the art we're after?" Lauren was losing her patience.

Slick Frankie placed his hand on his chest. "Let's just say for the sake of argument that I may have heard about some art objects affiliated with your man Lord—perhaps even the ones you mention—coming into the hands of certain people. Beyond that, all I can say is, mum's the word."

Slick Frankie held up his hand and looked at Lauren. "You're the reporter, right? Your job is to track down the story. So *you* figure it out." He glanced at his watch and whistled casually. "And with that, I must end our little tête-à-tête. I need to attend my grandson's Little League game in Cherry Hill. But before I depart the premises, I believe you, sir, were going to show me how much you appreciate me?"

"Well, I'm not going to be a party to this," Lauren said. She gestured to Sebastian. "When you finish your business you can find me in the gift shop. I'm going to buy souvenirs for my niece and nephew. Do you have anyone you want me to buy things for?" She arched her eyebrows.

He scowled. Last time his mother had called him—an occurrence about as frequent as a sighting of Halley's Comet—she'd said something about one of his stepsisters having a baby. "I think I have a stepniece—if there's such a thing."

Lauren was incredulous. "You don't know?"

"You should be ashamed," Slick Frankie admonished.

"Please, I don't need lessons in morality from someone whose activities are questionable at best— and that's just referring to you." Sebastian pointed at Lauren. "As for you—"

"I'm outta here." She waved goodbye and hastened down the hallway.

A few minutes later Lauren was paying at the cash register when Sebastian arrived. "Here. This is for you." She thrust a small package at his chest and stuffed another package into her bag.

Sebastian opened the wrapping and slowly lifted out a toddler-size T-shirt with the aquarium's logo. He turned it around several times before shifting his eyes to Lauren. "Not to question your judgment, but don't you think it's going to be a tight fit?"

"Please, it's for your stepniece, which you may or may not have." She didn't bother to wait as she headed out the door. "You know, it's statements like that that really make me wonder about you." She marched down the ramp circling around the seal pool. The parking lot was a five-minute walk, and it had started to sprinkle. She turned up the collar on her jacket and buried her chin in her chest.

"Great," she muttered. When it rained, her fine, straight hair became limp—wet noodle limp.

But for a change, it wasn't her hair that bothered her. It was the fact that Sebastian seemed so dislocated from family and friends. How could anyone be so isolated that they didn't even know their relatives? My God, there wasn't a christening or a wedding or a funeral in her family—and she meant her extended family, down to second cousins once removed—that she hadn't attended. Sometimes over her own dead body—slightly ironic in terms of the funerals—but then that was her problem.

Even more perplexing was why a man who did not know the extent of his own household was so concerned about returning artworks to their rightful homes. Something was missing in this equation. The man of mystery was only getting more mysterious with time. Frankly, it would have been a lot simpler if he had just remained a two-dimensional hunk. A warm-blooded sex toy. Someone to touch. And kiss. And lick...

"Earth to Lauren. Darlin', are you planning on walking back or would you like a lift?"

Lauren stopped and raised her head. Only then did she realize that she had walked right past Sebastian's parked car. He stood at the passenger side and held the door open for her.

"Sorry. I was thinking about the case and forgot

where I was." Well, it was kind of true. Sebastian was an integral part of what was going on.

"That's what I like about you—always on the job. And speaking of the job, Slick Frankie gave me the name of an antiques-cum-junk-dealer guy—he's a vendor at some big flea market in Lambertville."

Lauren nodded. "It's up in central Jersey, across the river from New Hope in Bucks County. A real tourist destination."

"That's what he said. Apparently the big day for horse-trading is Sunday, so he's sure to be there." Sebastian shut the door.

"Which means since tomorrow's Saturday, I'll have a chance to start going through the local missing persons claims and DOAs for the past six months," Lauren said when he got in the car. "That's about when you said Bernard Lord stopped picking up his benefits checks, right?"

Sebastian's cell phone rang. He stopped in the middle of slipping on his shoulder harness to answer it. "Excuse me. I'm expecting a call from the office in Washington."

He reached for his phone and flicked it open. "Alberti," he answered succinctly, then listened. "Yes, yes. I understand." He snapped the phone shut and put it away. He slanted her a narrow-eyed glance before starting the engine.

Lauren felt a cold front immediately engulf the car's interior. And it had nothing to do with the air-conditioning, which was off. "Something you wanna share?"

Sebastian pursed his lips. Placing his arm over

the back of her seat, he turned around to look behind him and backed out of the parking spot.

"That was Slick Frankie." He said finally, after shifting into first. His words were clipped. "He was a little confused. Something about your partner accosting him after we left." He slanted her a look, this one more critical than the last. "Something *you* want to share?"

"I don't know what you expect me to say. I haven't the faintest idea what he's talking about." Lauren ran a hand through her damp hair. "Don't tell me you don't trust me, yet again?"

Sebastian shifted the gear into second. "Sometimes I don't even trust myself."

8

THINGS ONLY GOT MORE frigid in the car as Sebastian pulled onto Riverside Drive.

It was really more than Lauren could stand. She was disappointed in him for not believing her, when she had thought they were past that stage. She was even more disgusted at herself for being disappointed that he didn't believe in her. The first was lame. The second was pathetic.

Best just to concentrate on getting the story. She was damned if she was going to have to keep justifying her behavior, let alone the behavior of others. "You're going to have to get on 676 South to get to 38 Roebling," she snapped. "Remember?"

"Who knows what will surface there? Our mystery caller?"

Lauren stared out the window. She refused to be baited. She was just hoping they'd uncover some information relevant to the story. Bernard Lord may have stopped going to the post office, but that didn't rule out the possibility that he had gone to ground. That he'd still be living on this street was probably too much to ask.

Oh, brother, was it.

Lauren and Sebastian didn't even bother to get

out of the car when they got there. Actually, "there" was something of a misnomer.

Lauren sighed. "Now I know why this address rang a bell."

"In this case, 'address' is a euphemistic term." Sebastian tapped his fingers on the wheel. "There is no 38 Roebling."

"Well, that's because there is no Roebling—at least, not anymore," she corrected.

He turned to her, his patience clearly stretched thin. "I think I can see that for myself."

"Two or three years ago, maybe more, there was an explosion in one of the buildings here. Seems the guys in some underground meth lab didn't quite heat their chemicals the right way. Ka-boom. It took out most of the block, and the few buildings remaining were severely damaged. The City fathers, in their ultimate wisdom, decided to raze the street with hopes of rejuvenating the area. Yadda, yadda, yadda."

Sebastian surveyed the wreckage. It looked like Dresden after the war. "Well, I think we can safely deduce that hope no longer springs eternal. I'll take you back to the hotel." He started up the car.

Lauren couldn't bear the thought of sitting in a hotel room with him. There was only one thing left to do—face an even greater evil—Friday family dinner. "Before you get carried away with driving, would you mind taking the Walt Whitman Bridge into the city instead of the Ben Franklin?" she asked.

"That seems a little out of the way."

"I've got an appointment in South Philly, and that puts me more in the general direction. It's not related to Bernard Lord's case. Trust me."

"You think after the phone call I just got I should trust you?" He negotiated the rush-hour traffic without breakign a sweat, despite the fact that Jersey drivers liked to tailgate within millimeters of the car in front, and turning signals were more an afterthought than a compulsory indication of shifting lanes. "Wherever you go, I go. Even if it's to hell."

"Truer words were never spoken." Lauren crossed her arms over her chest. "In that case, follow the signs for 76 East. And don't say I didn't warn you."

As soon as Sebastian pulled into an empty parking space on South Tenth Street—a true miracle if ever there was one—Lauren opened the car door.

"Auntie Laurie, Auntie Laurie, did you bring me anything?" A strapping eight-year-old girl banged open the screen door and tumbled down the steps of the row house.

What was once a modest neighborhood of brick row houses with high stoops was now an ode to aluminum siding and fake stone facades that were a big mistake even when they came into fashion in the fifties. Most of the residences had also sprouted enclosed front vestibules with delightful detailing like opaque glass louver windows. Lauren's parents' home was no different. Its particularly apt touch was the black metal silhouette of a coach and horses neatly screwed to the bottom of the white aluminum screen door. The only thing missing that would have completed the ambience was a miniature replica of the Rocky statue.

"Hi to you, too, Tabitha," Lauren returned the greeting.

Tabitha, sporting an oversize Villanova sweatshirt and baggy jeans, skidded to a halt in front of Sebastian's Mercedes. "Hey, way cool. Is it yours, Auntie Laurie?"

"Not quite. It belongs to Sebastian here. But if you want, after dinner he'll turn on the ignition and let you sit in the driver's seat. He'll even tell you about his John Deere tractor if you're very good."

Tabitha stared at Sebastian with a reverence that, in this neighborhood, was usually reserved for the Pope or the captain of the Philadelphia Flyers. "You have a tractor?" She practically choked on the words.

"Here, take this inside," Lauren said before Sebastian could speak. She thrust the shopping bag from the aquarium at Tabitha. "There's something for you and your brother—" Tabitha made a face at the mention of her brother "—I figure you'll know which is which."

Tabitha, no stranger to the right end of a present, scampered back up the steps and through the front door. Lauren turned to Sebastian. "Unlike most preteen girls, Tabitha is not a Britney Spears wannabe but a *Monster Garage* aficionado. You are now officially a god in her eyes. I'm sure that true wisdom will prevail when the hormones kick in."

Sebastian smoothed his tie with his hand and buttoned the middle button of his suit jacket. "*Monster Garage*? Auntie Laurie?"

"This way." Lauren motioned with her head for him to follow. "It's only going to get worse."

Lauren opened the front door and immediately heard Tabitha's less-than-dulcet tones. "Grammy, Pop Pop, Auntie Laurie's got a boyfriend."

Lauren glanced over her shoulder at Sebastian, who had noticeably blanched. "I told you."

"Tabitha, inside voice," came a soothing reminder from the kitchen in the back. And Lauren wondered why it hadn't occurred to her to suggest they stop at a bar and get a quick drink before coming. She also thought that Tabitha was probably right to shout, seeing as the Phillies baseball game on the television was turned up loud enough to drown out most civilized conversation.

Lauren slipped off her jacket and folded it over the newel post at the stair landing inside the door. She turned to the living room, where her father occupied his plaid recliner and her brother was hunched over the coffee table chowing down on Chex Mix.

"Hey, Dad." She bent down and kissed him on the cheek. Her father, a gnome of a man with the kind of blond hair that goes white with age, patted her forearm but kept his attention on the game. She raised her head and acknowledged her brother. "Carl."

"Who bunts with nobody on and no outs? Tell me, who?" Carl asked, gazing up at Lauren and stopping with his hand halfway to his mouth. His eyes quickly took a sharp left at Sebastian. He raised an inquiring chin. And munched.

Sebastian shrugged. "Other than Ricky Henderson in his glory days, and Juan Pierre and Kenny Lofton today, I'd say very few."

At that, Lauren's father looked up. Carl swallowed.

Lauren stood up straight. "Dad, Carl, this is

Sebastian Alberti, a colleague who's visiting from D.C. to work on a story with me. Sebastian, this is my father, George Jeffries, and my brother Carl."

George nodded. "Take off your jacket and tie and make yourself at home." He tipped his head at his son. "Make some room on the couch, Carl. And slow down on the nibbles. Your mother made a pot roast big enough to feed a Salvation Army gathering on Christmas Eve. Laurie, let your mother know there's an extra mouth to feed, and you can set a place at the table." He doled out the orders without missing the groundout to shortstop.

"I'm pleased to meet you, but really, I wouldn't want to impose on a family gathering," Sebastian said, attempting to back away gracefully. Sharks, fences, idiot managing editors and potential thieves—all these various sundries didn't seem to hold any terror. But the sight of one South Philly dad, and boy, did Sebastian look ready to hightail it in a hurry.

"Nonsense." George pointed to the couch. "You'll be doing me a favor. There is no way I can finish the pineapple upside-down cake myself, which would dearly sadden my wife, Alice. Sit."

Sebastian glanced at Lauren, who shrugged and made an I-told-you-so face. He shot back a you'll-pay-for-this stare. And succumbing to forces greater than he, Sebastian loosened his Zegna tie and faced the music. "As long as you're offering, I'd be mighty delighted."

Carl, his pale pink Ralph Lauren polo shirt stretched a little too tightly across his ample stomach, scooted down and passed Sebastian the bowl of party mix. Carl was an actuary who had left the old neighborhood and now lived in Kennett Square with his ever-expanding family and waistline. A true upscale suburbanite, he could afford mass-marketed designer pastels. "Just try and leave me the peanuts, okay?" he said personally to Sebastian.

Lauren shook her head at this display of male bonding and escaped to the kitchen.

Tabitha was running around her baby brother, who sat in a high chair methodically dropping peas onto the floor. "I'm a shark and I'm going to eat you," she shouted, pointing to her new T-shirt with a large shark jaw stenciled on the front. The baby squealed and only mildly objected when a tall and tired-looking woman placed the new hat Lauren had bought on his head. It had multicolored tentacles flopping in all directions.

Lauren came over and kissed the baby on his slobbery cheek. "Like the look, Teddy—a baby Rasta in the family."

"Just don't give him any reggae CDs, okay? I've got him listening to these overpriced Mozart-for-babies CDs, which are supposed to instill a love of classical music, as well as higher SAT scores, and I don't want the kid corrupted." This was from Teddy's mother and Lauren's sister-in-law, Maureen.

Lauren liked Maureen, even if she did make silly purchases. Originally, Lauren's mother hadn't been keen on the marriage but as soon as the first baby was born, those worries went out the window. Besides, at five foot seven, Maureen was expanding the Jeffries gene pool to maximize the chances of having the next generation of family members top the five-foot-four mark.

"Tabitha, stop running around and exciting your brother," Maureen ordered calmly. Or was it with exhaustion? Lauren wondered. Maureen was already expecting her third child, and at four months, she was starting to show a little tummy.

"Play in the backyard," Lauren's mother suggested as she closed the oven door and stood up. "Maybe you can pick some dandelions to put in a juice glass."

Lauren's mother was one of those immensely sensible women. Standing five-foot in her Rockport walking shoes, Alice Jeffries styled—styled was somewhat of an overstatement—her dark blond-gray haircut in a wash-and-wear pageboy. Over her wraparound jean skirt and lime green, long-sleeved polo shirt she wore a white butcher's apron. Indeed, Alice Jeffries' father *had* been a butcher.

"Okay, Grammy." And Tabitha took her random energy out the door.

"So who's the dreamboat you brought home?" Maureen inquired none-too-subtly.

Lauren opened a cabinet and reached for a dinner plate. "He's not my dreamboat. He's a colleague. We're investigating a story together, and since he was from out of town and had nowhere to go tonight, he came along." It wasn't an outright lie. She pulled out a drawer under the counter and grabbed an extra knife, fork and spoon.

"Well, let me get a look at your *colleague*." Maureen grabbed the plate and silverware and headed to the dining room table. Lauren's parents' house was set up railroad-car style, with the living room, dining room and kitchen laid out from front to back. The doorways for each room were also set in exactly the same relative position, so in just the right spot, you could look from the living room all the way to the kitchen.

"Maybe you could offer him a beer to get through the ordeal?" Lauren called out to Maureen's back. Sebastian chose that moment to angle his head around from the couch. He looked at her from beneath slanted brows.

"Your friend seems more than capable of taking care of himself. Why don't you chop the cucumbers for the salad," Lauren's mother announced from the stove. "They're on the counter by the sink. And do a carrot while you're at it."

Lauren walked over and pulled a paring knife out of a drawer. "He's just a visitor at the paper—someone I'm working with on a story." She laid a plastic cutting board on the counter.

Her mother turned her way. "No, take the white one. The yellow one is for chicken. I learned in *Good Housekeeping* that I should have a separate board for chicken."

Lauren did as she was told—one did not mess with the sacrosanct advice handed down from the mother of all women's magazines. She washed and rinsed the cucumbers, then began chopping them in the half-inch squares she knew her mother liked. "I know what I'm doing," she said when her mother came over and spied over her shoulder.

"It's not the chopping that worries me." Her mother glanced furtively over her shoulder before turning back to Lauren. She continued in a rushed whisper. "I heard from Ricky Volpe's mother about the apartment."

"Mo-om."

"Shh. I don't want your father to hear. You know how this type of thing upsets him. I just want to say I'm very happy you've temporarily moved into the hotel room with your friend—he *is* the one you're staying with at the Rittenhouse, right? He seems very levelheaded."

Lauren tightened her grip on the knife handle and mercilessly diced the next cucumber. "He's a colleague. It's not like I've moved in with him or anything."

"Really, Lauren." Her mother walked back to the stove. She picked up some pot holders and grabbed the handles of a large pot. "You'd think we were living in the Dark Ages. Gloria Hinkson's daughter has been living for years with that nice man who moved from Carnasie, and Rita's son—you remember Rita? I used to play bridge with her on Wednesday nights." She tipped the pot over the sink and drained the boiling water from the potatoes. "Well, her son is sharing this townhouse in Laurel, Maryland, with an older woman whose divorce hasn't been finalized. From what I understand, the townhouse is very nice, with brand new appliances in the kitchen and wall-to-wall carpeting in the bedrooms."

Lauren felt the beginning of a headache build behind her temples. With the sound of Maureen's footsteps on the linoleum floor, she breathed a sigh of relief. "Is Sebastian still alive?"

"He's perfectly fine. He and your father are talking about tomatoes," Maureen answered. She approached her pea-spattered son, who gave her a food-in-mouth smile. She wiped his mouth with the edge of his bib. "So, tell me, are you two sleeping together?"

Lauren nearly sliced off the tips of several fingers and nodded meaningfully toward her mother's back. Alice Jeffries might look like she was concentrating on mashing the potatoes, but Lauren wasn't fooled.

Maureen sidled over to her and wagged a dishtowel in Lauren's face. "I have one word for you—birth control."

"That's two words." Lauren started to chop again.

"No wonder I'm pregnant for the third time."

Lauren's mother looked up from furiously mashing the potatoes. "That's enough chopping, Lauren. Add them to the salad over there. Then put the bowl on the table along with the salad dressing."

As long as Lauren could remember, her mother made Thousand Island dressing from Hellmann's mayonnaise, ketchup and sweet pickle relish. The pink gelatinous goo held a special place in her heart. But then, Lauren had a big heart.

"After that you can come back and get the mashed potatoes and peas and pearl onions. Maureen, ask Carl to come in and carry the pot roast." Alice held her up with her hand. "On the way to the living room, you can bring in the gravy and the rolls. And call in Tabitha when you come back," she called after Maureen.

"Do I have to?" Maureen asked in a way that seemed to be only partly in jest.

Then Alice Jeffries turned to little Teddy and performed that ritual relished by grandmothers round the world—she scrunched her nose up behind his ear and breathed in fully. "My beautiful baby boy, you come with your Grammy." And she bent down to slide him out of the high chair before turning to glare at Lauren. "Well, are you just going to stand there?"

Lauren put the cucumbers in the bowl, grabbed the dressing and followed her mother into the dining room.

"Alice," Lauren's father said to his wife when she entered the room with her grandson in her arms, "did you know that Sebastian has a farm in central Pennsylvania?"

"No, I didn't know that, George." Lauren's mother bounced baby Teddy up and down on her hip. "You're a farmer then, too?"

Sebastian joined the group standing around the table. He'd shed his jacket and tie, and his French cuffs were haphazardly rolled up to his elbows. "I own a farm but I don't get there nearly as often as I'd like," he replied.

Lauren lowered the salad bowl onto one of the flower-shaped woven trivets that her mother had used since the dawn of time. "When you said you had a place in the country, I just assumed it was a cozy weekend retreat, and that owning a tractor was some kind of manly affection—something to go with a plaid shirt and fly-fishing gear. I mean, I never pictured you actually farming!"

Alice thrust Teddy into Sebastian's arms. "Why don't you hold the baby while I get the high chair?"

Sebastian stiffly gripped him by the stomach and bottom. He looked about as comfortable as if he were cradling a large quantity of plastic explosive. "Why not let me get the high chair?" he volunteered.

"Lauren, you shouldn't question Sebastian that way," Lauren's father chided. "You can tell by talking to him that he's a hands-on person, that he works his farm when he has the chance. Of course, like most people who run their own businesses, he uses help where he needs it. Look at me. I may be at the cleaners every day, but I still have hired many people—loyal people."

"Pop, loyalty is not the first quality I'd use to describe some of the people you've hired," Lauren interjected. "I seem to recall their weird doings provided steady fodder for my childhood diaries."

"Loyalty ranks above any personal quirks some of them may have displayed," her father said with the assurance of someone who'd had many years of Jesuit schooling. "Family and friends—what else is more important in life?" George Jeffries held his arms out for his grandson. "Here, let me take the little fellow. He can be a handful if you're not used to him." On cue, baby Teddy started bending both knees like a bullfrog ready to catapult himself across the room.

Lauren decided she'd had enough of trying to figure out why she agreed with her father about the importance of family and friends when they disagreed about so much else. Instead she directed Sebastian to a chair and grilled him. "So how come the rest of my family knows more about you than I do?"

"Somehow I didn't think biographical information was what you had in mind last night," he replied in a low voice.

"Lauren, where're the potatoes and the vegetables?" Alice Jeffries asked, bringing in the high chair.

Which gave Lauren a good excuse to escape before everyone could see she was blushing.

"Tabitha, wash your hands," Maureen ordered, and turned as Lauren entered the kitchen. "Look, Carl, your sister's blushing."

"I am not." Lauren grabbed the bowls of vegetables. "Ouch. Hot, hot." She quickly set them down and grabbed some pot holders.

Carl hefted the platter of meat. He moved past Lauren. "You are flushed, Lauren. Are you sick or something?"

Maureen scooted aside for her daughter to rush to the table. "I'd blush too if I had that 'something.'"

Lauren pursed her lips and tried to look superior. Not an easy task when she had her hands thrust into oversize oven mitts in the shape of pigs, but she tried nonetheless.

She pushed her way to the dining room table, where the family had left her an empty seat next to Sebastian—subtlety was never a Jeffries family trait—and set the vegetables on the remaining trivets.

"Finally," her mother huffed. "Now we can give Sebastian some fine home cooking."

"Mom, Sebastian is Italian. I'm sure he's used to home cooking," Lauren protested as she pulled out her chair. Sebastian stood and helped her push it closer to the table, an act eagerly noticed under her mother's eagle eye.

"Actually, growing up I lived more on microwave hot dogs and frozen dinners," he answered.

"Your mother didn't cook?" Lauren's mother appeared truly dismayed. As someone who measured her love by the amount of butter she put in food, she *was* truly dismayed, Lauren knew. It was a good thing her family didn't suffer from high cholesterol.

"My parents divorced not long after we moved to Alabama, and I lived with my father."

"George, give Sebastian an extra helping of pot roast. And make sure you have some mashed potatoes." Alice pressed the bowl into Sebastian's hands in an effort to make up for years of faulty eating.

"So you mentioned earlier that you were in art investigation. How does it work exactly?" Carl asked. He passed the baby his teaspoon and let him bang it on the high chair.

Sebastian took his share of potatoes and passed the bowl to Lauren, who was debating whether she should have some or not if she was going to fit into the pair of jeans that she had planned to wear tomorrow. "I work for an organization that tracks down artwork, whether it was misappropriated during World War II or stolen more recently. We also work a lot with museums to assure legitimate provenance for pieces that they've acquired over the years," he explained.

"Now that's the kind of thing you should write about—fancy things like art. Think of the high-class people you'd meet," her mother chimed in.

Lauren thought about Slick Frankie. So much for high-class. "I meet all sorts of interesting people on my beat, too." What the hell, she took a dollop of potatoes.

Her mother waved her hand. "Not that I know much about art, mind you. My family was more into wallpaper." It was true. The current paisley print on the walls of the dining room was a truly misguided cross between William Morris and Peter Max. The living room boasted an equally dubious choice of gigantic cabbage roses. You didn't want to see the bathroom. Lauren's mother was a serial wallpaperer—every few years, every flat, vertical surface in the house was redone.

"You know, if you really want to investigate art around here, Lauren should show you Petrucchio's. It's got the whole bay of Naples painted on one wall. Amazing," Maureen said. She motioned to Tabitha to eat her vegetables.

Lauren put down her fork. "I don't think Sebastian needs to see Countess Street."

Sebastian took a roll from Maureen's outstretched arm. "Petrucchio's?"

"It's the local luncheonette," Maureen explained.

"Where I wined and dined my lovely wife-to-be during our courtship," Carl added, picking up the spoon that baby Teddy had dropped on the floor for the tenth time.

"More like stuffed me with cheesesteaks," Maureen corrected good-naturedly. "Boy, was I easy."

Sebastian looked at Lauren sideways. "Maybe I should take you to Petrucchio's?"

Lauren's headache just kicked up a notch.

Her mother beamed. "Art. Isn't it wonderful! And to think it brought you to our neighborhood. Now have some more meat, Sebastian."

9

BY THE TIME THEY'D finished dinner, the button on Lauren's pants was digging into her waist so much she thought she might be in the process of acquiring a second belly button. Then there was her headache. It had marched across the width of her forehead and now seemed lodged on either side of her jaw.

Sebastian, on the other hand, appeared to perk up as the meal went on. Or maybe it was just the sugar rush from two pieces of pineapple upside-down cake.

Now, as she watched him hold Tabitha on his lap while he revved the Mercedes' engine, she began to feel a certain sense of relief that the evening would soon end.

"He's a good fellow. Sensible," her father said, standing next to her on the sidewalk outside the house.

Lauren shifted the foil-wrapped dessert leftovers to the other hand. "What's that supposed to mean, Pop?" As if she couldn't guess.

"Now don't get all riled up. I know you think I'm going to lecture you about getting married, and I'm not saying I don't want to see you with a husband

and family, mind you. But despite what you may think, your mother and I are very proud of you, of all you've accomplished with your career. Did you know she keeps clippings of all the articles you've ever written?"

Lauren nearly squished the pineapple upside-down cake. Nearly. "You're kidding me? That must take up a ridiculous amount of space."

Her father chuckled. "Why do you think we had to give you all those boxes with your old stuff to take to your new apartment? There was no space in your old room anymore to keep the things."

Lauren sniffed. "And here I thought Mom was just getting ready for a new wallpapering project before she started on my place."

Her father rested a hand on her arm. "I know about the break-in." He held her still when she started to say something. "I heard about it from Bruno Cremelli, who plays handball with Ricky Volpe's father. Now listen, I'm not going to tell your mother. You know how this type of thing would upset her. But what I meant about Sebastian—him being sensible and all—will you take his advice in this matter? About if and when it's safe to move back in?"

For some absolutely ridiculous reason, Lauren felt tears well up in her eyes. Rather than lose it in front of her father—something that hadn't happened since the swim coach in high school told her that she was bumped from the relay team—she concentrated on Tabitha and the wonders of a well-tuned V6 engine.

"All right, time to wrap up the start of the Daytona 500 here," she called out when she felt more in control. "I promised Phoebe we'd be there an hour ago." Okay, so she'd exaggerated. "As it is, it's going to take us at least twenty minutes to drive to Boathouse Row." Vesper Boat Club was one of several rowing clubs located among the quaint boathouses that lined the Schuylkill River.

Sebastian turned off the engine and passed an awestruck Tabitha to her grandfather. He got out of the car. "Far be it for me to disappoint a lovely lady such as Phoebe."

"You've met Lauren's friend, Phoebe, I take it?" Lauren's father asked. "A real Main Line glamour gal, like Grace Kelly, only more so," he said, referring to the late local golden girl who'd gone on to become Princess Grace of Monaco.

"She's definitely what we in the South would call a belle of the ball, though myself, I tend to prefer them shorter and more low-key." Sebastian gazed momentarily at Lauren before turning back to her father. "George, it's been a pleasure meeting you." He took his hand out of his pocket and offered a handshake. "Please thank Alice for the wonderful supper. You've got a delightful family."

George returned the handshake. "Anytime. And if you need your suits cleaned and pressed while you're in town, be sure to bring them by the store. We'll take good care of them, for free."

Lauren was in shock. Never had she heard her father speak those two words—"for free"—before. It was definitely time to leave, even if it meant bodily prying the adoring Tabitha away from Sebastian's right leg.

The relief that washed over her when they finally got in the car, and when her family went back in the house, was palpable.

Sebastian waited for her to put on her seat belt. "I thought that went rather well, don't you think?" He paused. "Lauren, are you hyperventilating, or are you just trying to express how much you yearn for my body?"

She held up her hands and panted loudly. "I'll be better in a minute. I just need to recover from our up-close-and-personal encounter with my family."

He chuckled. "I see what you mean. My calf is still going into spasms where Tabitha gripped it. The kid should be a weight lifter."

"She adores you, you know." *They all do*, she said silently.

He waited a moment before he spoke. "What's really wrong, Lauren?" Sebastian asked softly. He shifted to face her straight on.

"Nothing." *Everything*, she thought. She was starting to realize that the rest of her family wasn't alone in their feelings. Which was absurd, absolutely ridiculous—and undeniably true. Now he seemed genuinely concerned, but she couldn't forget the anger he had shown when he'd thought she was deceiving him. She entwined her fingers together on her lap and worried a cuticle with a thumbnail.

Sebastian rested a hand on hers. "Did Phoebe really invite you to go out tonight?"

Lauren wondered if he felt the rays of heat pass between his hand to hers. "Yes. Actually she extended the invitation to both of us. It's a soirée to raise money for the preservation of colonial herbal gardens or something else equally historical and Philadelphia society-like." She braved a glance at his face.

"Maybe we can skip the soirée?" He let go of her hand and guided his fingertips to the back of her neck, gently massaging it.

One thing for sure—all his earlier hostility seemed a distant memory. "You think?" She closed her eyes. "Oh, that feels sooo good. Promise me you'll tell me if I start to drool."

Instead he lowered his head and brushed her lips—in desperate need of Chap Stick, she immediately realized and then just as soon forgot—with his. The contact was as light as clichéd gossamer wings, but as penetrating as a hydraulic drill. Lauren felt her insides dissolve and bubble up—and it had nothing to do with an overdose of gravy and mashed potatoes.

He pulled back and she opened her fluttering eyes. "You were drooling. I had to do something," Sebastian explained.

Lauren swallowed and worked to keep her heart from pounding with so much force that it threatened to implode. "Tell me one thing. Have you changed your mind about me being an art thief?" Her body told her one thing, but she had to be sure with her heart.

Sebastian studied her face, moving from her eyes to her mouth. Yes, definitely lingering on her mouth, before moving back to her eyes. "After tonight, I've decided there's no way for you to be an art thief without your whole family knowing everything about it—and everything else in your life, for that matter. And that includes your sister-in-law, Maureen. She managed to slip a packet of condoms into a pocket of my trousers and made a point of letting me know that Johnny Budworth was a total creep—her words not mine—and that you deserved better."

Lauren picked a piece of nonexistent lint off her pants. "You sure she wasn't just trying to cop a quick feel. It's being pregnant, you see. Her hormones are raging."

Sebastian bit back a smile. "And here I thought it was my overwhelming charm." Lauren snorted softly—well, not that softly. "Mock me, but I got to tell you, your brother Carl also pulled me aside—"

"He gave you condoms, as well?" Lauren was stunned.

Sebastian ran the back of his finger along her jaw. "No, he wanted to let me know that he wasn't going to tell your parents about the break-in."

Lauren wet her lips as his gentle touch moved closer to her mouth. "No need, they already know."

He cupped her chin. "I rest my case."

She peered down at his hand. "But what if the whole family is really a bunch of art thieves? What if they're all in on it? Tell me your suspicious mind hasn't considered that?"

He angled his head and brushed his face against her hair. "Please, with your mother's taste in wallpaper, there is no way she would recognize a Caravaggio let alone works by Nicola Pisano."

Lauren inhaled his scent, his heat, him. "You're

right. Did you see how she even wallpapered the refrigerator?"

"I didn't want to say anything, but yes. Please tell me you're not going to let her have a free hand with your apartment?" He pulled away to look at her.

Lauren grinned. "She has been wanting to take me to paint and wallpaper stores, but so far I've begged off."

"Well, be polite but stand firm." He kissed her lightly on the lips, then resettled into the driver's seat and put on his seat belt. He glanced at her and waited. In the glow of the street lamps, his dark brown eyes seemed larger, darker. Frankly, hot.

She had a feeling her own blue eyes were also larger, darker. Frankly, hot. And it wasn't just her eyes. "I tell you what, why don't you pull out from the curb and do a U-turn. Then take a left at the light. That'll take us to the hotel in twenty minutes or so."

"And then what happens?"

"I promise you, we won't be saving herb gardens."

IT TOOK SEBASTIAN FIFTEEN. But then the traffic lights had been in his favor, and he also got the first parking space in the garage.

"You know what I like about you?" Lauren asked outside his hotel room.

"That I pick up my dirty laundry?" Sebastian unlocked the door.

She stepped over the threshold and set down the doggy bag of cake. Her insides were jumping around so randomly, she was sure that at any moment her spleen would merge with her appendix, causing a rupture of cataclysmic proportions.

"That's an important factor, but not what I had in mind." She was still able to talk, so her organs must not have shifted too much. Other things were definitely shifting, however.

He tossed his keys on the side table and flipped on the lamp. "So there's something else I excel at?" he asked slyly. It was becoming difficult to walk, impossible to think, he wanted her so much.

She grinned back. "Why, it's your uncanny ability to get the best parking space. You seem to find the right spot anywhere, anytime. Anyplace." She rested her hand on his lapel.

He raised his chin. "What about now?"

She loosened the knot of his tie. "I'd say right now you've got the best spot in the house."

Sebastian placed a hand on top of hers. "Then how about a reward for all my troubles?"

"Reward?"

"I was thinking along the lines of a tie for a tie?"

Lauren's fingers itched under the weight of his. "Tell me more."

"It's like this— I take off my tie, then you take off yours."

"The only problem is, I don't have a tie."

"Well, then we'll just have to improvise, won't we?" His look was an open invitation.

And she took it. Then and there, she yanked off his tie. And didn't bother to wait as she feverishly worked at undoing his buttons.

"Hey, you're getting ahead of me," Sebastian protested. So far, he'd managed to wrest off her jacket, spilling the contents of one pocket and slightly tearing the lining at the shoulder.

"You're objecting? Jeez, did you have to wear a shirt with so many buttons?" She was having tremendous difficulty unfastening the damn thing.

"All right, go ahead. Rip away."

She stopped momentarily and looked up. "Are you crazy? This is a custom-made shirt. I can't just 'rip away,' as you so blithely put it."

"Forget the cost. To quote Engelbert Humperdinck, that god of seventies lounge singers, 'release me.'"

And she did. Every last button popped off and sailed across various parts of the carpet.

And somehow they ended up on the carpet, as well. Sebastian without his jacket, tie and shirt, Lauren clothed in her bra and pants. They kicked off their shoes—and she kicked him in the process. Only he didn't seem to mind. Not with his hand unzipping her trousers and his fingers snaking between her legs to find the silky material of her panties, already moist with desire.

Come to think of it, she didn't mind, either. Lauren struggled with the zipper of his pants and managed to get it halfway down before she lost total patience and just plunged her hand inside. She pushed down his boxers and eagerly found his engorged penis. She ran her hands up and down its length.

Sebastian hissed. He shimmied out of his pants and underwear and helped Lauren lose the rest of her clothes. Stopping only to grab a foil packet, he rolled on the condom and positioned himself above her naked body. He looked into her eyes, then bent down and suckled one nipple.

Lauren bucked from the floor.

He switched to the other breast. She started to moan. He put his hand between her legs and, with his thumb working her clitoris, plunged a finger deep inside her, removed it, and plunged again.

It started. The intense buildup that seized her body and sent it careening over the edge. She felt her muscles repeatedly spasm with a force that left her senseless, blocking out all light, all sound. She knew she was crying out his name, but she couldn't hear anything coming out of her lips.

All she knew was that she wanted him, all of him, inside her now, together. She grabbed his hips and forced him to lower his pelvis. "With me. I want you now," she moved her lips, begging—yes, begging—that he could hear her.

And he did, entering her in one thrust. He pulled back, but she didn't want him to. She raised her hips in search of his heat, his fire. "Don't hold back," she called out in a strangled cry.

And he didn't. He moved into her over and over, somehow deeper, harder, merging every sensation, every fiber of their bodies, and every element of their souls. And just when the intensity seemed to be too great, and Lauren was tempted to hold back, Sebastian found her throbbing center once more and penetrated a final time.

The result was sheer anguish coupled with over-the-top bliss. It was like floating and crashing all at the same time, simultaneously an out-of-body experience and an overwhelming internal awakening.

She was losing it, totally. And she wanted more. More of Sebastian.

If her body was ever capable of functioning again, that was.

He fell, exhausted, on her chest—their moist skin meeting, squeaking as they touched, their chests rising and falling with each forced breath.

He nuzzled her behind her ear and bonelessly patted her hair. "Just promise me one thing." He inhaled deliberately.

Lauren found her eyelids stuck together and gently pried them apart. "I'm not sure I can deliver anything at the moment, but what?"

Sebastian flopped his hand to the carpet. "Just be sure you never tell anyone that I quoted Engelbert Humperdinck while in the throes of passion."

10

"SO WHAT ARE YOU UP TO this morning?" Sebastian toyed with a few strands of Lauren's hair. She lay on her back next to him, her head resting on a pillow, her eyes shut. Despite appearances, he knew she was awake—because of the smile on her face. And because of what they had just done that had put that smile there. He had no doubt that the same pleased-as-punch-I-could-just-lie-here-all-day glow was affixed to his mug, as well.

He propped himself up on an elbow and enjoyed the view. In the early morning light, Lauren's pale skin achieved a translucent glow, and her fine bones had the grace and delicacy of a Renaissance oil painting by Duccio—the high cheekbones, the fluid arch of small brows, the pointed chin, the swanlike neck. Except, she wasn't carefully applied colors on a wooden panel, but flesh and blood. She was giving and gentle, fiercely competitive and cooperative at the same time. Their lovemaking only accentuated the contradictions. Three times they had come together, twice in a fervent heat, once in a slow, tortuous languor. And one of those times they had made highly inventive use of the pineapple upside-down cake—upside-down had been the operative word, in fact.

Maybe the sex *did* have something to do with the way he was feeling now. But it wasn't all. It was also the revelation of who Lauren was.

She was street smart and intelligent as hell, but she *was* innocent—and not just regarding the crime. For the first time, he had met a woman who was true blue, genuinely good—with a mouth, mind you, but down-to-the-core pure.

She was an angel with an attitude, an attitude that she could take on the world no matter what. Look at the way she coped with the aftermath of the fire and the break-in at her apartment.

But the thing of it was, her very disdain for neediness under circumstances that cried out for help, also underscored her vulnerability—the same vulnerability that had gotten to him from the get-go.

That vulnerability made him want to reach out and outline her cheekbones—which he did just now—and cradle her chin—which he did, as well. It was a feeling of sweetness, of intimacy, that was completely distant to him, but as welcome as his childhood memory of sitting under a vine-covered pergola and dipping crusty chunks of warm bread into freshly pressed olive oil.

It felt like…it felt like home, which was absurd here in a hotel room in a strange city with a strange woman who somehow wasn't strange—mysterious and inviting, but not strange at all.

So when she smiled and opened her eyes, eyes that conveyed sated desire, Sebastian smiled back, proud that he was the one who had put that look there. "So what are your plans for the day, Sleeping Beauty?" he asked again.

At his appellation for her, Lauren blushed slightly. She reached out and lightly stroked his bare chest, its hard contour of muscles and dark hair now so familiar to her. "Other than letting you have your way with me, I was planning on hitting the records office at the Center City precinct—you know, what I said yesterday about checking up on the missing persons and DOAs. Pretty tedious stuff really, but who knows, I may get lucky."

"You think they're just going to open up their files to you?"

She cocked an eyebrow. "You don't know the half of my persuasive powers." What was it about being with Sebastian that brought out a sense of sexy playfulness in her? It wasn't as if she'd been a sexual novice before they met. But she'd never considered herself a flirt, let alone a vamp, by any means. That's what this affair had done for her—helped her discover her inner vamp. Lauren wet her lips and smiled more broadly.

"Only the half of your persuasive powers, you say, darlin'?" Sebastian locked his eyes on her luscious lips and skimmed her collarbone with the back of his fingers. "It's not for lack of trying, I assure you."

His touch felt so good that Lauren let her head sink sideways into the pillow. Which actually gave her a great view of the alarm clock, a sleek Alessi number—naturally, only the finest in design for the Rittenhouse. Reluctantly, she stilled his hand. If he didn't stop what he was doing, they would likely be here until the next leap year. "As delightful as this is—and to salve your male ego, it truly is delightful—I've really got to get up and face the music."

She let go and swung to the side of the bed.

"So you really think you'll find something at the station?" he asked without moving.

She ran a hand through her hair, succeeding in mussing it up even more. It was all Sebastian could do not to yank her back and ravish her once again. "I don't know. But it's worth a try, and, yeah, I'm pretty sure I can get access to the records—having grown up with half the beat cops and met the remaining ones during my years on Metro."

She looked back over her shoulder. The sheet rode low over Sebastian's stomach, and she had no trouble imagining what lay beneath. No trouble at all. She sighed and rose to her feet, bravely pretending it was no big deal to stand naked in broad daylight in front of the watchful eyes of an Adonis. Especially when she was sure the stretch marks on her hips, left over from her days as a chubbette, were still faintly visible.

"You can stay here you know," she said with a calm she certainly wasn't feeling. "It's bound to be pretty boring, and I know you have other things to follow up on. That phone call from eastern Europe in the middle of the night sounded urgent."

His damn contact in Zadar never could calculate the time difference correctly. "No, it can wait." In truth it couldn't—according to his source, a cache of stolen Russian icons was waiting on the docks ready to be shipped out to Malaysia and from there, to points unknown. He really needed to get a warrant to search the boat, and put a guard in place immediately to make sure the goods didn't do a disappearing act.

All that took haggling, along with deep pockets and the knowledge of whose palms to grease. He'd have to get the job done. He usually did. But this time it'd have to fit in with other things.

Things like the car that had followed them from Lauren's parents' home back to the hotel. It had stayed too far away for him to get a read on the make, other than to tell it was a dark compact car with Pennsylvania plates. Now, more than ever, he was convinced that the break-in at her apartment hadn't been some random act of urban crime.

Given Lauren's stubbornness, he figured it was prudent not to tell her. He had no doubt she would refuse to curtail her activities despite the threat. No, the best thing was to keep her in his sights—here at the hotel and on the street.

He rose from the other side of the bed. "Actually, I think I'll come along with you. You know what they say about two pairs of eyes being better than one? Besides, I want to be there to fend off any advances from those members of Philadelphia's finest who feel duty-bound to replace your infamous fiancé."

Lauren waved off his comments. "Please, they are so out of the picture."

Her words shouldn't have mattered. They did. Oh, boy, did they.

"And as to my fiancé—he wasn't so much infamous as unmemorable. I look on that period of my life as one of relative growth—I grew into adulthood while he regressed into self-absorption."

"So why did you get engaged?"

"Because he asked. Because he was from the

neighborhood, and I felt like somehow I was retaining the comfort of home. You know." She shrugged and entered the bathroom without waiting for a reply.

Sebastian stood and listened to her turn on the shower. "No, actually I don't," he answered to the empty space. But he had more pressing matters to deal with than the lingering hollowness in his stomach, the same hollowness that had followed him around all his life and that he had gotten used to ignoring.

"SO, DARLIN', YOU MIND telling me why I get the suspicious look and the reluctant handshake, while Detective Zagarola practically lifts you off the ground with a bear hug?" Sebastian asked, sitting in a swivel chair next to Lauren. "I know, say it. He played football for your high school."

"Actually, he threw shot put for the track and field team. Besides, he was just being nice."

"Nice was not how I'd describe the way he looked at you."

"Don't be ridiculous. He's married with kids. Besides, I think it was the six boxes of Girl Scout cookies I ordered from his daughter's troop that got him to agree to let us track down information."

"Trust me, you could have bought a whole case of Thin Mints and it wouldn't have had a fraction of the impact compared to the tight jeans you're wearing."

Lauren bit back a smile and continued to scroll through the files on the computer screen. So it had been worth struggling into them this morning when

Sebastian was in the shower—not so much for the detective's reaction as for Sebastian's.

It was awful, she knew, but there was something highly flattering about having a man display a little jealousy. She had a feeling it wasn't a quality that Sebastian was prone to. She turned to him and grinned, finding herself charmed in the middle of a room with bad fluorescent lighting, cracked linoleum tiles and computers older than even the *Sentinel*'s. "You know, Alberti, there isn't anyone I'd rather be searching DOAs with."

He offered her a slight smile. "All right, but I still want half the cookies."

Lauren rubbed her upper lip and enjoyed staring at Sebastian's smiling face for one more lingering moment before getting back to work.

Since Harry Nord—the real Harry Nord—would have been physically incapable of carrying out a delicate heist, she zeroed in on Bernard Lord. The files showed that in the six months since Lord last collected his veteran's check, there had been four unidentified male DOAs. Two floaters—one in the Delaware, the other favoring the Schuylkill—a gunshot victim minus a head, and one body recovered in various bits and pieces due to the misfortune of having been crushed in a car compactor. One of the drowning victims was identified as over fifty, the other drowning and the headless guy most likely in their twenties. The jury was still out on the bits-and-pieces guy. In other words, just your usual walk in the park. Come to think of it, there weren't any fatalities in the parks in that period.

"The older victim might be Lord." Lauren

glanced over at Sebastian, who sat in a chair next to her. She jotted down the case number in her notebook.

He nodded. "Possibly. I'll check with the VA to see if I can obtain dental records—however dated they might be. If we're lucky—not that I believe in luck—we'll get a match."

"Sounds good. Meanwhile, let's check out the missing persons." Lauren closed the one program the way the detective had instructed her and called up the other on missing persons.

This one contained more names over the same time period. After slogging through about eleven weeks, Lauren's stomach began growling loudly.

Sebastian leaned closer, his mouth close to her ear. "Hungry?" Under the desk, he placed his hand on her thigh.

Even through her jeans, she felt the warmth of his touch. She surveyed him through half-closed eyes. "Starved."

Sebastian grinned. "Anything I could do to abate your hunger?"

"What I have in mind would never be a blue plate special, let alone come from the frozen food aisle of the supermarket." She leered.

Lauren sat up straight. Had she just leered? She must have, because Sebastian was leering back.

He bent forward—

And his cell phone rang.

He rolled his eyes. "I've got to take this call, but hold that thought." He planted a quick kiss on her lips and rising, flipped open his phone.

Lauren followed his back with her eyes as he

moved away for privacy. Making out in a police station was definitely a novel experience.

She sighed and stared blankly at the computer screen. She could easily get used to doing all sorts of things with Sebastian Alberti, she realized—all too easily. She held her eyes shut and deliberately reopened them. The words still swam on the monitor—except for one that jumped out at her like a sumo wrestler on skates.

Or a small, middle-aged lady in Rockports with appalling taste in wallpaper.

Alice Jeffries had filed a missing persons claim four months ago regarding a Benny Lord. Benny? Bernard? It was too close to be a coincidence. Lauren jerked her head around to see if Sebastian was still occupied on the phone. He was pacing in the small office and didn't see her. She shifted back to the computer and quickly jotted down the information.

There was no way in hell she was going to share what she'd just found—not right now at least. She needed to check it out—alone. She wouldn't be so much hiding evidence, she reasoned, as trying to put it in context. No good reporter went off half-cocked, right?

Lauren wiped her suddenly sweaty palms.

Even though Sebastian had sworn that she was no longer under suspicion, Lauren had a sense of foreboding that something like this could tip the balance against her—yet again. She didn't want to fight him. Not because she wasn't ready to defend herself, but because it was a lot harder to mount the good fight when all you really wanted was respect from the other party. She had waged that kind of long-running battle with her parents. She didn't want to do it with Sebastian.

No, the best thing to do was to give him the information when she knew more and was better able to control his reactions. She forced herself to examine the remaining files.

She was finishing off the rest of the otherwise uneventful entries when Sebastian rejoined her. "Find anything positive?" he asked.

Lauren shook her head. "Nothing I'd call positive." The understatement of the year! "What about you? Your call?"

He cocked his head. "The usual bribing of corrupt officials, foiling the bad guys and restoring religious art treasures to their rightful home. Just an average day."

"Well, you may call it average, but I think it calls for some well-deserved public glory. Please say you'll let me write the story for the wire services?"

Sebastian sliced his hand through the air. "No stories. The commission likes to solve things quietly, without fanfare—all the better to infiltrate underground organizations and cultivate contacts without blowing anyone's cover."

"Well, if you can't enjoy public glory, how about a little celebration?" She desperately welcomed a change in focus from Bernard Lord and now—she gulped—quite possibly Benny Lord.

"I'm already on top of it." Sebastian pulled his hand from behind his back. "You said you were hungry, and this was the best I could muster from the vending machines in the hallway." He placed a bag of Doritos and a can of Dr. Pepper on the desk next to the terminal.

"Doritos I can definitely handle, but Dr. Pepper? You are showing your southern roots, Alberti."

"You've got something against Dr. Pepper?" he asked with sincere outrage. "Why, sugar, Dr. Pepper is the elixir of the gods." He hunched down next to her. "Tell you what, though."

"What's that?" Lauren swiftly closed her notebook without taking her eyes off his face.

"How about I show you something else from the South that's just as sweet and even more satisfying?"

Lauren slipped her notebook into her bag. It was hard to flirt when her anxiety level was at an all-time high.

He brought his head down to hers and, brushing aside her hair, licked the skin on the back of her neck with the tip of his tongue.

Lauren cleared her throat and straightened up. "I guess I could use something to go with the chips."

See, it wasn't that hard after all.

"WHEN I OFFERED TO ENGAGE in illicit activities, this is not exactly what I had in mind." Sebastian locked the door to the car and watched Lauren head into Elwood's Tattoos and Piercings, next to her apartment. Sebastian had found a parking space on the street, right in front. Naturally.

Lauren shrugged off his complaints. "You should learn to expand your horizons, Sebastian. Anyway, as I told you, when I checked my voice mail this morning, my landlord left a message that he'd left a set of keys to the new locks with Elwood. Surely you can delay tripping the light fantastic for a few minutes while I pick them up and check that they work."

Given the unspecified danger Lauren was in, Sebastian thought the decision to leave the keys to her apartment with the proprietor of a tattoo parlor showed poor judgment at best, a real threat at worst. He scowled as he crossed the sidewalk and stepped behind her. She pulled open the door to the store, and they were immediately assaulted by heavy metal music.

Elwood, all three hundred and twenty pounds of him, sat behind the counter. His black hair was in dreads and he wore a jean jacket with the sleeves cut out, all the better to display the barbed wire tattoo around the gleaming mahogany skin of his upper left arm. He looked up from reading the *New York Review of Books*. "Yo, Lauren baby, what's up? You finally decide to get that belly button ring after all? Just in time for spring and all those sexy bare midriffs."

"Glad to see you're up on your fashion trends, Elwood, but I'm still not ready to make the commitment," Lauren apologized. "But if I do, I'll definitely come to you first."

"What about your friend here?" Elwood nodded toward Sebastian and surveyed him critically. "Nipple rings really turn the women on, you know."

Sebastian plunged his hands into the pockets of his buttery-soft, dark brown leather jacket. "Do you think I need help?"

Elwood cocked an eyebrow and laughed

abruptly. "Hey, can't fault a man for trying to do business. No problems, man." He nodded to Lauren. "So if you're not here to discuss the newest John Updike book, either, I suppose that leaves the keys that your sorry-ass landlord left me." He unlocked the register and lifted the bill tray. "If you ask me, he'd be better off investing in a security system and a couple of rottweilers. I don't like the idea of you alone up there."

Lauren took the keys. "You sound like my mother."

Elwood held up his hands. "Hey, don't knock mothers. I always listen to mine."

Lauren made a face and glanced at Sebastian. "Say, handsome, you coming up?"

"I'll be with you in a minute. I just need to get some change from your neighbor here for the meter." Sebastian waited for her to go out the door, then turned to Elwood. "You see anything the day of the break-in that might have been related?"

Elwood shook his head. "Like I told the cops, *nada*. This neighborhood gets a lot of foot traffic, so there're people coming and going all the time."

"What about since then? Anyone hanging around more than usual?"

"Sorry, not really." Elwood made a stop sign with one enormous hand. "One thing, though. Earlier today, I saw this white dude who I hadn't seen before outside her building. He wasn't doing anything, didn't try the lock, if you catch my drift. But I didn't like him hanging out, so I stepped outside and made my presence known. When he saw me staring at him, he made this big deal about asking if I did Hells Angels tats."

"I'm sure you've gotten that request before."

"Not from someone in a JC Penney blazer and orthopedic shoes."

Sebastian removed his hands from his pockets. So much for Mr. Casual. "Can you describe him, other than the clothes?"

Elwood shrugged. "That's the thing of it—I've never seen a more average dude in my life. Twenties, maybe thirties, medium height, brown hair. Looked like he hadn't ever seen the inside of a gym."

"You didn't happen to notice a car, did you? A dark compact?"

"Sorry, I had other customers come in, so I didn't get a chance to see where he went after he left the store." Elwood paused. "Listen, I hear your concern. Rest assured, anyone messes with Lauren, and I might be forced to do something nasty. You know what I mean?"

Sebastian nodded. "I know exactly what you mean." He rapped the countertop with his knuckles. "Thanks. Listen, here's my card with my cell number on it. You hear or see anything suspicious, you call me, okay—and that's before ringing 911."

Elwood studied Sebastian's business card before slipping it into the chest pocket of his vest. "Gotcha." He hit the transaction button on the register. "Here."

Sebastian frowned in confusion.

"Change for the parking meter—on the house. Take care of her."

Sebastian took the change and left, only slightly relieved. Earlier at the police station, he'd sensed

Lauren's tension, and he was worried she might have realized that this case was putting her in jeopardy. He hated that, hated not being able to do something to stop the perpetrator, hated to see the worry that she hid with that smart-alecky bravado of hers. Going back to her apartment for the first time after the crime was only going to exacerbate that anxiety.

He loaded the meter with some quarters and looked up and down the street. That's when he spotted the store across the way. He might not be able to lay his hand on the criminal or criminals at this very moment, but maybe he could do something about the worry in Lauren's eyes.

"YOU REALLY SHOULDN'T leave your apartment open this way," Sebastian said, pushing aside Lauren's slightly ajar front door. He stopped when he found her kneeling next to packing boxes on the floor.

She looked up, emotion visible in her eyes. "I thought since I needed to buzz people in at the front door it was just easier. But you're right, I should be more careful."

Sebastian inhaled deeply. He didn't mind being right. He just didn't like being right when it clearly made her sadder than she already was.

She lifted the lid of one box and rummaged through it. "If the thief had walked off with these, I wouldn't have had to bother unpacking them. Would you look at all this stuff my parents sent over?"

He wasn't sure if she meant the question as a real one, but placing the shopping bag he was holding on the floor, he squatted down and peered inside. "What's that?" he asked. There was a pale blue book with gold embossing wedged into the side.

Lauren reached down and took it out of the box. "Oh, God, my old diary." She laughed with a shrug and opened the book from the back. "This is so embarrassing—all this preadolescent angst. I used to pour out my heart about the injustice of not being one of the popular girls—my extra roll of fat around the middle immediately cut me out of the 'in' crowd, you see. Other things, like ambition, probably didn't help, either."

"Their loss, believe me," Sebastian said.

"Oh, I haven't suffered any long-lasting trauma." Lauren randomly leafed through the pages. "Geez, would you look at this. I wrote that my family sailed on a boat through the Suez Canal. The ferry to Cape May, I'd believe—but definitely not Egypt. That is so typical. I was manic about writing every day, but when there really wasn't anything going on, I kind of made up things, embellished them. Somehow it made life more exciting, I don't know, rosier." She stared limply at the page—reading but not reading.

Sebastian reached over and took the book and gently placed it on the floor before taking her hands in his. "Oh, *bella*, I wish I could make it all go away, but I can't."

Lauren stared at her small hands engulfed in his. She swallowed with difficulty and realized that this was the first time Sebastian had ever spoken to her in Italian. It was only one word, but sweet. Kind.

She had been prepared to steel herself against coming back and facing the mess. Sweetness and kindness were a whole other kettle of fish. She dropped her chin to her chest. "I feel so violated."

"I know." He wrapped his arms around her and kissed her gently on the forehead. "It's perfectly natural to be upset, to feel scared. But from now on, I'm not going to let anything happen to you. I promise."

Lauren's eyes were watery and on the verge of overflowing. She lifted her head up. "I'm used to taking care of myself, you know. I'd never ask you to protect me."

"I know. Your determination and ability to take care of yourself are probably your most attractive attributes." He pulled back, his arms still encircling her, and did a quick up-and-down survey. "Well, two of your most attractive attributes."

Lauren wiped her eyes and shook her head. "You are such a bullshit artist."

"*Au contraire.* As both a native Italian and an adopted Southerner, it's merely my natural charm."

This time Lauren laughed. "Dream on."

He lifted the corner of his mouth, producing a sexy dimple in his cheek. And Lauren remembered all over again just how blown away she'd been by his good looks that first time at the press conference. "It's a good thing I have a healthy male ego," he joked.

According to all logic, she should have been too worried about why her mother was mixed up with Benny Lord, and what relation—if any—Benny had to Bernard to indulge in sexual bantering. But logic seemed to have flown out the window.

Lauren turned her attention downward, raised

her eyebrows, then looked up. Sebastian may have relaxed his grip, but their bodies still fit together snugly. "That's not all that's healthy," she observed.

His grin widened. "Which is highly convenient, darlin', because I have just the cure for what ails you—and me." He reached behind him and grabbed the shopping bag by the handles.

Lauren noticed the large purchase for the first time. "Shopping? You're talking about shopping?"

"I've always been a great admirer of your deductive capabilities, Lauren, but this time you are sorely lacking." He placed the bag between them. "Here, a present for you."

She frowned and opened the bag. "They're sheets." She picked up the top packet and skimmed the label. "Sebastian, you fool, these are Pratesi sheets. Where did you get them?"

"At the store across the street." He rose and proceeded to pick her up in his arms, shopping bag and all. Well, there were muscles under those designer clothes of his, after all.

"Sebastian, these are incredibly expensive, and nobody goes into that store who doesn't vacation in Biarritz and drive a Mercedes. Oh, I forgot—you drive a Mercedes. You've probably been to Biarritz, too."

He eased her down onto a chair in her bedroom and started stripping her bed.

She clutched the shopping bag. "What do you think you're doing?"

He gathered her sheets into a ball and put them in the laundry hamper he found in her closet. "I'm attempting to erase the bad memories and replace them with new ones—unforgettable ones, I hope."

He walked over, dipping his hand into the shopping bag, and dug out the package with the bottom sheet. He ripped it open and handed her the cellophane wrapper.

Lauren looked at the label, mystified. "According to what's printed here, these are made of seven hundred count Egyptian cotton material."

"Soft as silk, yet wears like iron, according to the saleswoman." Sebastian glanced up from slipping the fourth fitted corner on the mattress. "Toss me the top sheet, will you?"

She poked through the bag. "You want me to help?"

"No, I've got it under control. I'm trying to impress you with my domestic skills, you see."

Lauren blinked and furrowed her brow. She shifted the bag on her lap and pulled out the pillow slips. "They're a beautiful color, by the way. Kind of a pale peachy rose."

Sebastian snapped the top sheet open and let it flutter over the bed. He bent over and smoothed it flat. "I thought so." He looked up and stopped. "It's the color your skin turns when you're aroused."

Lauren stopped breathing. And felt her cheeks start to blossom in that very same color. "Really, Sebastian, this is too generous a gift. I couldn't possibly sleep on these."

"I wasn't planning on you sleeping."

And it was with a package of pillowcases in one hand and a too, too chic shopping bag on her lap that Lauren Jeffries fell in love. And it had nothing to do with the invitation to have sex.

Well, that didn't hurt.

11

"HERE YOU GO, LAUREN, a little something to quell your hunger." Phoebe held out a foot-long hot dog that glowed an iridescent pink, even in daylight. Its paper wrapper probably contained more organic ingredients than the hot dog, let alone the roll on which it rested.

Lauren slanted Sebastian a critical look. He was the one who'd gone with Phoebe to the food tent at the Lambertville Flea Market. "I thought I could trust you when I said I wanted something to eat," she said ruefully. "I was thinking more along the lines of coffee and a bagel."

He shrugged. "She assured me you loved the taste of nitrates in the morning."

Lauren had no qualms about swiping his cup of coffee. "Don't bother protesting." She reluctantly took the hot dog from Phoebe's mitts. "Next time remind me not to leave you in charge of the food when I have to hit the little girls' room," she lectured her friend. "Come to think of it, maybe there won't be a next time."

Phoebe blinked slowly, hardly the image of contrition. "Pshaw. You're the one who should feel guilty about standing *me* up the other night. Without you there, I was forced to spend the evening drinking truly mediocre white wine—why people insist on supporting Argentinean vintners is really beyond me. The least you could do was let me come along on a drive in the country. Besides, we can all sing show tunes on the way back."

Lauren was hoping that suggestion would die if she ignored it.

"So rather than cramp the style of you two intrepid investigators and, dare I say, lovebirds—" Phoebe truly had no shame "—I'll be off on my own." She looked at her vintage Cartier tank watch—the perfect accessory to her white wool crepe pants, Tod driving shoes and Jackie O sunglasses. "In about an hour from now I'll come looking for you. In the meantime, I am so in the mood for tchotchkes." She waved her fingertips.

"Don't you just love it when the Mayflower maiden speaks Yiddish?" Lauren asked Sebastian.

"Tell me again why we let her come along," Sebastian said as he and Lauren watched Phoebe stride off, shoulders back, arms swinging and hips swaying.

Lauren shook her head. "I think it has something to do with her undying support and fearsome slap shot. So who's the guy Slick Frankie told us to look for?" She handed him back the coffee. "You can have it, after all."

He took the paper cup. "That bad, huh?" He took a sip and shivered, then dumped the container in the nearest trash bin. "According to Frankie the Fence, we are in search of Vincent the Vendor—a specialist in porcelain and fine china." He locked his arm through Lauren's elbow. "Come, my lovebird."

Lauren let her arm rest comfortably in Sebastian's and adjusted her steps to his long, relaxed gait. If one didn't know any better, it would be easy to think they *were* a couple.

If she didn't know any better, *she* could easily think they were a couple.

"So other than looking for a Limoges imprint, do we have anything else to track Vincent down?" she asked.

Sebastian guided them through the crowds bunched at the various tables and open truck beds. Everything from old LPs and crystal jewelry, to ancient farm equipment and World War II memorabilia was on display. "Frankie said our man was medium height, brown hair, on the paunchy side." The fact that the description wasn't all that different from the one Elwood had given him at the tattoo parlor wasn't lost on him. Instinctively, he gripped her arm more tightly.

The first china table they came to was run by two middle-aged women wearing cable-knit sweaters. A pair of corgis were tied up to a lawn chair. Sebastian and Lauren looked at each other and moved on.

But at the far end of the field, wedged between an aging hippie selling dashikis and incense and a man in a clown costume hawking comic books, they found their man.

Sebastian caught his eye when he made a show of examining what was supposedly a Minton soup tureen.

"I can see you have a discerning eye, sir. That's quite a nice piece." Vincent exuded enough bonhomie to coat several stacks of pancakes.

Sebastian replaced the lid on the bowl. "Actually, it's not quite what I was after. A colleague of yours named Slick Frankie said you might be able to help me with what I'm really looking for."

Vincent's smile vanished. "I'm a little busy today. Maybe you could give me your name and number and I could get back to you?"

"Maybe I could report the fact that you're selling cheap knock-offs for the price of the real thing?" Sebastian looked him steadily in the eye.

Vincent shifted his stance. "I suppose I have a few minutes."

"I thought you might." Sebastian pulled out the photo of Bernard Lord from his leather jacket and held it up. "Look like anyone you may have come across, accounting for the fact that he may have been a good deal older than he is in this picture?"

Vincent bent forward and squinted. The man definitely needed reading glasses. "Could be. What's his name?"

"Lord, Bernard Lord," Lauren answered.

Vincent glanced straight at Lauren's boobs before shifting his attention back to Sebastian. "I don't know about a Bernard Lord, but the guy I know who looks like this—much older of course—goes by the name of Benny."

"Just Benny? No last name?" Sebastian asked.

"No, just the one—like Cher."

"What else can you tell us about Benny besides his name?" Lauren inquired, her voice muted. She wanted to know more and, at the same time, was afraid at what she might hear, especially since she hadn't been able to get through to her mother. Last night, when she and Sebastian had gone to dinner at Sansom Street Oyster House, she'd tried to call from the ladies' room, only to remember that her parents were at the Phillies game. And this morning, things had been so rushed and Sebastian constantly within earshot, she wasn't able to try again.

"What else can I tell you about Benny?" Vincent repeated in an annoying singsong fashion. "Not much, except that he was a nice enough guy, brought me stuff on a sporadic basis, some of which I bought, some I didn't. You could say he had eclectic tastes."

"Tastes that ran high-end?" Sebastian asked this time.

Vincent sucked in his cheeks. "How high-end?"

"Very high-end. Specifically, a piece of Carolingian silver, some Renaissance candlesticks, a small painting by Caravaggio."

Vincent ran his hand through his thinning hair. "High-end is a bit of an understatement, don't you think? Even if he brought me that kind of stuff— which he didn't—it's not exactly my market. Look around! Besides, I don't mind closing an eye for things like Hummel figures, but what you're talking about is way out of my league."

Sebastian snorted.

Vincent shrugged and pointed to the photo. "Funny thing is, I think even old Benny did, too— have scruples, I mean. A couple of times he came back to me all sheepish, asking to buy back the stuff he'd sold me—like he maybe had second thoughts about how he'd acquired the goods. I sold them back to him, naturally, at a higher cost."

"Naturally." Lauren's disdain was barely concealed.

"Well, I am a businessman, after all," Vincent defended himself. When he saw that other customers were approaching his table, he straightened up and affixed his smarmy smile.

"One more thing." Sebastian stopped him before he could move on. "You keep using the past tense when you talk about this Benny character. Hasn't he been around lately?"

"Nah, not for at least half a year. But then, guys like that, who knows? He could be hanging out at the dog tracks in Hialeah for all I know."

"Oh, I almost forgot." Sebastian leaned over the table and placed his hand on top of the large tureen. One careless move, and the whole thing would topple on the ground. "You mind telling me where you were all day Friday?"

Vincent focused on Sebastian's hand before looking up. "I was right here at the flea market. Ask any of the other vendors around." He raised his chin and walked away, honing in on the couple who were examining some teacups.

Phoebe came sweeping in on Sebastian's left. "Any luck, my dears, cracking the case of the Man-Who-Never-Was-But-Actually-May-Have-Been?"

"Perhaps," he answered. "Our charming representative here from the Better Business Bureau recognized the photo but identified him as a certain Benny, not Bernard Lord. And the name Harry Nord never even came up, which just confirms our earlier suspicion that the real Harry Nord—not the fictitious one in Lauren's obit—was never part of the picture. So this Benny may or may not be our man. And in any case, we still don't have a lead as to where he is now." He turned to Lauren for the first time since interrogating the vendor. "What do you think?"

"My God, Lauren, you're as white as a ghost," Phoebe exclaimed. "Are you having an allergic reaction to that hot dog?"

Sebastian gripped her by the shoulders. "Are you all right? I'm pretty sure his alibi will hold, and he's not the one who broke into your apartment, if that's what's worrying you."

She shook her head. "No, it's not that. It's just—just that I think I might know where to look for Bernard Lord—definitely not the real Harry Nord—but most likely Benny."

They looked at her, stunned.

She gulped. "The dry cleaners."

OVER PHOEBE'S PROTESTS, they dropped her off at her apartment in the Fairmont section of Philadelphia. "Trust me, I think it's for the best," Lauren assured her as she transferred to the front seat in the car. "This could get ugly."

Phoebe clutched her Hermès bag to her side. "Well, call me if you need moral support."

Sebastian waited until Lauren had settled in the car. "Now where?"

"The hotel. There're some things I need to check first." She could tell Sebastian wanted to say something. But he didn't. And she could tell he wasn't happy. With the situation *and* with her.

When they got to the room, Lauren searched

around quickly. "I'm pretty sure I brought it back from the apartment yesterday. For nostalgia's sake."

Sebastian frowned. "Can I at least help with whatever you're looking for?"

"It's my old diary. Here it is." It was on the bedside table. She sat down, picked up the book and quickly thumbed through the pages. "This is the section." She read a few pages and looked up. "It's what I was afraid of."

Sebastian walked over to her in measured steps. He waited.

And Lauren knew she would have to be the one to break the silence. "Remember how I told you I sometimes embellished the truth in my diaries?" He nodded. "And how the other night I made a joke about the weird employees at the family dry cleaners and how I used to like to write about them?"

"I remember, and then your father made a big deal about worker loyalty." Sebastian didn't sit next to her. Instead he stood, his tall figure looming over her small, seated one.

Lauren felt defensive. Who wouldn't? And she knew that was Sebastian's intent. "Well, there was one fellow in particular who used to work for us, an old guy, very quiet. He worked the pressers upstairs and was especially good with delicate fabrics. Things like wedding gowns were his specialty."

"And all this is leading to...?"

"In a minute, please. Anyway, every once in a while after school, I'd go upstairs at the shop and find some wedding dresses there to be cleaned and pressed. I'd very carefully try on some of them—you know, fantasize about one day being a bride."

Sebastian raised an eyebrow. "If you say so. I'm still not seeing how this all relates to the case."

She held up her hand. "You see, when I did that, I'd sometimes get to talking with this guy, who I used to call Uncle Ben, because he had short tufts of white hair, a little like long grain kernels of rice. And sometimes Uncle Ben would even talk to me— about things he'd done or places he'd been. He told me how he'd served in World War II, and that he'd been shot down over Italy.

"And here—" she pointed to the pages open on her lap "—you can see where I jotted some of it down. I wrote about how this brave flyer's plane went down over Italy, and I went on and on about how despite his severe wounds, he managed to rescue another member of the crew. And that they hid out in this Italian village, finally escaping to safety by hiking over the Alps."

She looked down at the entry. "Here I wrote about how they'd hiked 'in the extreme cold and record snowfalls, with the aid of nothing more than a compass and a flask of brandy.' Obviously, my imagination added all kinds of made-up details to the stories he told me. And my imagination and my old memory trick of using words that sound alike contributed to the fake obit. Uncle Ben. Benny Lord. Harry Nord."

She raised her head to size up Sebastian's reaction. She watched him work his jaw.

He took his hands out of his jacket pockets. "All right, I see the similarities between your diary entry and the obit. And, who knows, in a pique of anger, one could even argue that you conjured up your childhood flights of fancy and incorporated your tales of Uncle Ben into the obit. But that still doesn't prove that this Uncle Ben is Bernard Lord or even Benny for that matter."

"There's more." She walked over to the desk and picked up her minicassette recorder. "On Friday, when we met with Slick Frankie at the Camden Aquarium, I recorded it."

"You never told me."

"I know, maybe I should have." This was only the beginning of her confession. "It was in my bag, so you wouldn't have known. Anyway, do you recall how I pressed him for more details on who exactly had the stolen art, and he said, 'Mum's the word'— that I was the reporter, so I should go find out?"

"I don't need a recording to remember that he clammed up."

"But do you also remember that just before he said goodbye, he started whistling this tune?"

Sebastian nodded. "I vaguely remember that."

"Do you remember what it was?"

"Not particularly," he admitted.

"Well, at the time, I didn't think it was anything important. But the more I thought about it, the more I realized it was. Anyhow, just listen." Lauren fast-forwarded to the relevant section of the tape, where Frankie was whistling, and let it play. Then she hit Rewind and played it again. "Ring any bells?"

"Should it?"

"It's 'Oh, Dem Gold Slippers.'"

"So?"

"That's the Mummers' theme song," she answered. "The Mummers are huge in Philly, what with the weird costumes and the New Year's Day parade. In fact, there's even a Mummers Museum in South Philly—and it's a really big deal."

Sebastian frowned. "I'm not sure where all this is leading."

"Don't you see? He was giving me clues—'mum' for Mummers, the song. He was trying to tell me that the art was actually here in Philadelphia, South Philadelphia in particular."

"I don't know. That's a pretty big stretch."

"Not when you consider this, as well." She pulled her notebook from her bag and walked over to Sebastian. Opening it to the last page with handwriting, she pointed to her jottings. "Four months ago there was a missing persons claim filed for one Benny Lord." She stopped. "The claim was filed by Alice Jeffries."

For more than a minute there was this eerie silence. When Sebastian did speak, his voice was unnaturally controlled. "And you didn't think to tell me about this yesterday at the station house?"

"Of course I thought about telling you yesterday, but I was worried how you'd react."

"And how was that, precisely?" His voice grew louder.

"That you'd immediately assume that my family was involved along with me, or, barring that, that I knew they were involved but was trying to cover it up."

Sebastian averted his eyes. "That only begins to sum up what I'm thinking." He pulled out his cell phone and handed it to her. "Call your mother."

Lauren wanted to refuse, simply because she

didn't like him ordering her around. But she also knew it was the logical next step. The only step. If this thing was going to get cleared up, they needed to do something now.

She punched in the number and waited. "Hi, Mom, it's Lauren," she said when her mother picked up the phone. "I was wondering if Sebastian and I could come over? What's that? We're at the hotel, so it will take fifteen, twenty minutes, okay? Actually, no, I wasn't planning on looking at the wallpaper samples, but if you really want me to... Yeah, another time in early morning light would probably be better. Good, we'll see you soon then."

She disconnected and handed the phone back to Sebastian. "Satisfied?"

He was already grabbing his keys. "Let's hit the road."

"Hold on a sec." Lauren went over to check her bag.

"Suddenly discovering yet another piece of evidence?" he asked sarcastically, his hand on the room door.

Lauren pulled out a sheet of Pepto-Bismol tablets. The way her stomach was feeling, she was a poster child for acid reflux disease. "I just need to chew a few of these." Who was she kidding? Probably the whole load of them couldn't quell the rumbling in her gut.

And it had nothing to do with the foot-long hot dog.

12

THE FOUR OF THEM—Lauren, Sebastian, her mother and father—sat around the Formica kitchen table. Despite Lauren's protests, her mother had insisted on serving coffee and a sour cream coffee cake. Nothing like carbohydrates and caffeine for a last supper.

Lauren looked back and forth between her parents. She didn't dare steal a glance at Sebastian, who sat stonily at the end of the table. "Mom, Pop, did you guys ever have an employee at the cleaners named Benny? I vaguely remember this old guy working the presses."

Lauren's father, rested his fork on the side of his plate. "Sure, Benny Lord. Great detail man—very good with embroidery, beadwork, you name it."

Sebastian leaned forward. "Does he still work for you?"

George shook his head. "No, he's been retired for some years now. Besides getting old, he had a small problem with the bottle, wasn't always reliable. We tried to get him to join AA, even had Father O'Phelan talk to him. He'd go to the meetings, but it wouldn't last. A sad case. But other than his few failings—and who of us is to judge—he was a loyal employee, and I valued that above all else."

Lauren clenched her hands. Loyalty, trust—qualities Sebastian wouldn't know about, she realized. What had she been thinking when she'd fallen head over heels in love with him, anyway? She hadn't been thinking, that's what.

"Was Benny's real name Bernard?" Lauren asked.

Her father rubbed his chin. "It might have been Bernard once upon a time, but you cut the check to Benny Lord, right, Alice?"

"That's right, I keep all the books, and I distinctly remember listing him as Benny Lord in all the accounts," his wife agreed.

Lauren cleared her throat. "When was the last time either of you ran into him?"

Her parents looked at each other. Her father shrugged. Her mother stretched her lips in a thin line. She turned to Lauren. "It's been a while. Less than a year, I think. You see, even after he stopped working for us, he'd still come around every once in a while. I always tried to give him a little something—not that he asked outright, mind you."

Lauren wet her lips. "Mom, did you file a missing persons report on him about four months ago?"

Her father gave her mother a surprised look. Alice nervously folded her hands. "Yes, I did. I was worried. Benny was old. He didn't have any family as far as I knew. It wasn't like him not to stop by the shop at least once a month or so." She looked anxiously at Lauren and Sebastian.

Lauren smiled reassuringly.

Sebastian crossed his legs. Reassuring was not how she'd characterize his body language—not by a long shot. "You mentioned 'a *few* failings' that Benny had, George? Were there others besides the drinking?" he asked.

Again her parents darted glances at each other. George patted his wife's hands and turned to Sebastian. "Benny had a problem, the kind of problem that could get him in trouble. But everyone on the street, all the businesses where my shop is located, understood it and tolerated it. We knew he couldn't help himself, and that he actually felt terribly guilty about the whole thing. He would try to make it up afterward by giving us all little presents. But like the alcohol, it seemed to get the better of him from time to time."

"What exactly was his problem?" Sebastian pressed.

George opened his hands. "Benny was a kleptomaniac. He walked off with things, not big ones, mind you. Sometimes a coffee mug from Petrucchio's, the luncheonette opposite the cleaners. Other times, I'd find stuff like buttons and zippers missing from m place. No big deal."

Lauren pushed aside her uneaten coffee cake and rested her forearms on the table. "We think Benny was into a little more than buttons and zippers, Pop."

Her mother moaned. "Oh, now I see. I told you, George. That Hummel figure he gave me one Christmas was too good to be true. Can I return it to someone? I feel just awful."

Lauren placed her hand on her mother's linked ones. "No, Mom, don't worry about the Hummel figure."

"What we're interested in is worth more than one hundred thousand Hummel figures," Sebastian announced.

Her mother gasped. Her father blindly searched for his coffee cup.

"Mom, Pop, we're trying to track down four works of art, four valuable works of art that Benny may have stolen," Lauren said, trying to sound as sympathetic as possible. She had a feeling if it weren't for her presence, Sebastian would have turned on a high-intensity lamp.

"Four *extremely* valuable works of art," Sebastian amended. He didn't need a lamp.

"We know nothing of art, valuable or not," George protested. Her mother gripped her fingers harder.

"Well, maybe you've seen these things without even realizing it?" Lauren suggested. "You know how these things can happen."

Sebastian raised his eyebrows.

"Maybe," her mother conceded.

Lauren edged her chair closer to the table. "Okay, one of them is this silver chalice, this big wine cup, like for Communion."

Lauren's parents frowned in thought, and then Alice turned to her husband. "You don't think she could be referring to that old black and dented thing that Julius uses? Didn't Benny give it to him after he'd taken a few roses for the homeless lady by the branch library, I don't know, at least ten years, no, maybe fifteen years ago?"

Sebastian uncrossed his legs and sat forward. "Never mind the roses. Who is Julius?"

George nodded. "Julius is the florist on my block at work. And you could be right, Alice. He has this cuplike thing that he uses to keep pennies in so people don't need to worry about making change. But it's all black and dented. It could really use polishing."

Sebastian waved his hand. "Never mind the wear and tear. Can you give me the phone number and address?"

"Of course. I don't see why not," George said. "Alice, you've got it in your little book, right?"

She rose from the table and pulled out a narrow drawer under the counter by the wall phone.

"Mom, Pop, there's also this painting, Italian, not too big."

"According to church records, it depicts St. Lawrence as he's being martyred over an open fire," Sebastian elaborated.

Lauren's mother sat back down at the table and placed her address book in front of her. "Oh, that creepy dark thing? It scared people so much that Tony, the owner of Petrucchio's, finally hung it in the men's room. His wife kept nagging him to put it out in a garage sale, but you know Tony—he can never part with anything."

Sebastian looked wide-eyed at Lauren.

"Mom, can you put Tony's number down, too?"

"There are two other things still missing, actually more like a pair," Sebastian said. "Two large matching candlesticks, in marble, very ornate, also Italian."

Alice frowned. "Candlesticks."

"I'm pretty sure that Rosenbaum's Funeral Parlor has this really gaudy candlestick standing next to the organ," George said.

"You're right," Alice agreed. "Really awful, something my grandmother would have had in her house."

"And when did they start displaying it...also about fifteen years ago?" Sebastian asked.

Alice squinted. "That would be about right."

"Now think. Did Benny happen to take a trip to Italy some time before these objects began to appear?" Lauren pressed her chin forward.

George rubbed his thumbs and index fingers thoughtfully. "Actually, a little before all this, Benny went on a tour organized by some World War II veterans' group. You know, the kind of trip where soldiers visit the scenes of old battles. Some of these trips go to Normandy, others Anzio. In Benny's case, it was northern Italy."

Alice Jeffries touched her husband's hand. "I remember now. We were all so excited that Benny was showing interest in being with other people. We had a little going-away party for him, and Sadie Rosenbaum even made a sponge cake. And then, when you and Tony went to pick him up at the airport when he came home, you practically threw your back out lifting his suitcases—he'd bought so many souvenirs."

Lauren sat up. "That's right. He gave me a plastic Leaning Tower of Pisa. I loved it. I remember keeping it on my dresser for years. I wonder where it is now?"

"I think you'll find it in the bottom of one of the boxes I sent over to your apartment," her mother said proudly. "I found it on a shelf in your closet under the pressed corsage from your senior prom. The corsage I didn't save, though, too faded."

Sebastian held up his hand. "Let's forget the plastic Leaning Towers of Pisa and the faded corsages for a moment if we could. We still have one candlestick unaccounted for." He shifted his head back and forth between George and Alice.

"It seems to me that Benny might have offered us one about the same time, I guess," Alice admitted.

Sebastian peered around the room. "You mean it's here in the house?"

"No, no," Alice corrected. "He gave it to you at the shop, George, and when you wanted to bring it home I wouldn't let you. Don't you remember?"

"You're right. And I remember how that thing had a way of kicking around the cleaners for years."

"So where is it now?" Lauren asked.

Her parents frowned. "I'm sorry, I just can't remember, Lauren," her mother apologized.

She focused on her father.

"Neither can I," he said. "We used to use it as a doorstop for a while, but beyond that, my memory draws a blank. It was so long ago. For all I know, we could have thrown it out."

Sebastian slumped back in his chair. "Well, I suppose three out of four isn't bad—if indeed they *are* the objects we're looking for."

Lauren narrowed her eyes. "You and I *both* know they will be. There's no such thing as coincidence." She paused. "And seeing as we're going to be in the neighborhood, Pop, do you think we could search through the cleaners? Who knows, the second candlestick may be hidden somewhere, like in the fur storage vault."

"Of course, dear. Your mother can write the security code down with the phone numbers for the others. In fact, if you want, I'll call everybody and get them to come in and show you the things you mentioned."

Sebastian rose and stretched his legs. "I'd appreciate that. The sooner I can wrap up this case, the better I'll feel. The objects were taken from a church in Italy, and I'd like to return them to their rightful home as soon as possible."

"To think, a church," her mother echoed. "Please don't tell me they were missing a Hummel figure, as well."

"AT LEAST CAN YOU AGREE that my parents weren't involved in any crime? I mean, now what Slick Frankie was hinting at becomes perfectly clear. Nobody—not my parents, not the rest of the shopkeepers on Countess Street—had any concept of the value of the stuff," Lauren argued.

They had just come out of Rosenbaum's Funeral Parlor, where, as in the case of the luncheonette *and* the florist, they had hit pay dirt. It was surprising how heavy a candlestick could be, Lauren thought, as she lugged it in a canvas tote bag that Sebastian had stored in the trunk of his car.

He'd insisted they keep the items with them at all times, despite the car's security system, which meant wrapping the painting in bubble paper and a blanket—also from the car—and holding it under his arm. He covered the chalice with paper and carried it in a shopping bag in the other hand.

"Wittingly or unwittingly, your parents—along with the other people on the block—didn't report a crime, a major crime," Sebastian answered as they waited between parked cars for the traffic to clear so they could cross. Even though it was Sunday, people came to South Philly to shop and stroll and eat out.

"But no one knew the items were stolen, let alone how valuable. You saw how stricken they all looked. Mr. Rosenbaum had his arms raised, wrists locked together, when we arrived at the funeral home. He was ready for you to cuff him and haul him off to jail." She rested the tote bag against a dark blue sedan and watched the cars go by.

When a break in the traffic opened up, she hoisted the bag and headed across the street. "Pop's place is down half a block."

Sebastian easily kept pace despite having his hands full, and when they got to the cleaners, he waited for her to remove the key from her pocket. Over the shopfront was a black wooden sign with gold scripted lettering. He frowned in confusion. "Jeffries French Dry Cleaning? I didn't know Jeffries was a French name."

"It's not." Lauren pushed open the door with her shoulder. "French dry cleaning is a technical term. It means using petroleum solvents and doing most of the pressing by hand." She turned off the alarm system on the wall.

She swung the tote bag onto the counter and leaned forward, resting her weight on two hands.

How many times had she struck this pose growing up, helping out in the store?

She looked at the low ceiling and the paneled walls, taking in the pricing chart and the calendar from Ace Hardware with the photo of fluffy puppies rolling around. Nothing much had changed over the years except for the dates on the calendar. And it would probably remain the same until her father eventually retired. "Well, I can't say that I spy a Renaissance candlestick anywhere obvious."

Sebastian closed the front door and approached the customer side of the counter. "Then let's look in the not-so-obvious places." He set the two pieces he was carrying on the countertop and leaned his hip against the edge. Even in a leather jacket, well-worn jeans and a crewneck cashmere sweater cut like a sweatshirt, he appeared natty as all get out—and sexy as hell.

Lauren purposely looked away. She hated knowing how intensely attracted to him she still was, despite the fact that things on the personal front were clearly unraveling. "So where do you want to start? The back room of this floor or upstairs?"

"Let's start in the back and move up if necessary. I don't want to have to lug this stuff—" he pointed to the cache of reclaimed items "—all over kingdom come any more than necessary. Until I see these safely back to Italy, they're not leaving my sight." He balanced the painting under his arm and grabbed the bag with the chalice. "After you."

Lauren grunted as she lifted the bag and led the way through the doorway behind the counter. The back room contained cleaned clothes, hanging from racks in plastic bags, and giant cleaning containers. She rested the bag on a table and peered around the room.

Sebastian inspected the tanks. "What's in these—the cleaning chemicals?"

"Petroleum solvents," Lauren answered, standing straighter, "as opposed to the solvent percholoreothylene, or perc, that most cleaners use these days. They're more expensive and labor-intensive, needing to be distilled regularly to remove impurities. Not to mention highly flammable."

Sebastian prowled around the room. "So why bother?"

Lauren watched him disappear under the hanging clothes. "Because petroleum solvents are more gentle. They don't remove sequins or strip buttons—all the horrors of regular dry cleaning."

Sebastian reemerged. "Somehow I never realized dry cleaning was such a competitive business." He paused to look at Lauren, giving nothing away except an intensity of wanting to get the job done. "I don't see anything here. Would you mind showing me the upstairs?"

"Sure, why not?" She grabbed the handles of the canvas bag. "Let's take the side stairs. They go directly to a large room in the front with the pressers.

Sebastian followed behind, telling himself it was perfectly natural to notice the sway of her hips in her jeans. Certain things were meant to be admired, after all—fine wine, women's hips. This particular view of Lauren's backside corresponded to one of the great vintage years.

Never mind. Never mind that he felt like

gathering her up in his arms and trying to ease away the sadness that he read in the sag of her shoulders.

He knew she was hurting, but that wasn't his problem right now, he told himself as he trudged up the steep stairs. From the beginning, he had stated that his priority—his first and only priority—was to retrieve the stolen art objects. Whatever else they'd shared had been a fringe benefit—a mutually satisfying scratch of an admittedly large itch. Anything more was out of the question, especially after she'd purposely held back information on the case. That was tantamount to betrayal in his view. And one thing he had learned in life—betrayal cut to the bone. If anyone was bleeding, it was he.

Besides, it was clear that she had a veritable phalanx of admirers ready to help her lick whatever wounds she might be left with. He frowned. He didn't particularly want to think about those admirers, let alone thoughts of licking.

"We hand-finish most of the garments, using either steam pressers or hand ironing," Lauren explained when they reached the top stairs. She turned around and waited for him to join her.

Sebastian hesitated a moment before taking the final step. "Hand-finishing?" he asked, seemingly distracted.

"Yeah." Lauren swept her hand in the air like a practiced tour guide. "We use a large press for tablecloths, but things like tuxedo shirts are done by hand. And wedding gowns are entirely done by hand." She walked across the old wooden floor, a dim light from the day's end filtering through the large front windows. It provided a soft contrast to the bright fluorescent lights overhead.

Sebastian laid his packages on the large presser and slowly strolled around the open room. He studied the machinery, gently touching a corner here, a curve there.

Her stomach clenched. He did that a lot, she realized. Touched things. And she instantly remembered how those hands had touched her in so many places, so lovingly. She slowly lowered her bag to her feet.

Sebastian walked to a mannequin. "What's that for?"

"Oh, that's a Suzie." Lauren's voice was weary. Even if they found the missing candlestick, she doubted she'd feel the commensurate elation. "It's a mannequin-shaped presser. You use it for dresses and suits. Then a worker finishes up ironing the sleeves, collars and cuffs by hand."

Sebastian gave it a once-over, then turned to Lauren. "Well, the work area is clean and tidy, nothing out of the ordinary, no unwarranted clutter. You said there was a room where your mother keeps the books?"

She nodded. "Yeah, and a refrigerated fur closet—both in the back. I'll show you."

And she would have, except the overhead lights suddenly went out. She swore. "A circuit breaker must have tripped. Let me just run downstairs and turn it back on." In the increasingly graying light, she eased her way around the large presser and bumped into something.

Or rather, someone.

"MY GOD, HUEY, HOW DID you get in here?" She laid her hand on her chest.

"Through the front door. You conveniently left it unlocked."

Lauren stared at Sebastian in dismay. "That's right. I forgot you need the key to lock it." A light flickered near her hair and she pulled back. "Huey, what are you doing?"

"Shedding a little light on the matter," he snickered. The flame from the butane lighter cast his smirk in a ghoulish glow. "And here you thought I didn't know what alliteration was."

Lauren wisely decided not to explain that he hadn't used alliteration but a metaphor. "Well, be careful with that. It can be dangerous." She took a cautionary step back.

"That's not the only dangerous thing." Huey slid his other hand into the droopy pocket of his blazer. When he removed it, it wasn't empty.

Lauren's eyes opened wide. "Huey, that's a gun. Do you have a permit for that?"

Huey waved it back and forth. "I think that should be the least of your worries."

Sebastian slowly circled around the other side of the presser.

"No, hold it there." Huey waggled the .22 at Sebastian. "Hands up."

Sebastian obliged by raising his hands. "Deciding to do a little stealing yourself, Hugh?"

"More like scooping," Huey corrected Sebastian with a firm nod.

"What on earth are you talking about?" Lauren croaked. "You're after a story?"

Huey turned to her and waved his gun to indicate she should raise her hands, as well. She got them as far as her shoulders. "Can you think of a better reason? The whole paper—even Uncle Ray—thinks I'm incompetent, while little Miss Metro uncovers the story of the year. Well, not anymore. I've been listening and watching, you know—following you from the beginning. And I'm going to be the one to break open the case."

"So you're the one who broke into Lauren's apartment, who talked to Slick Frankie the Fence at the aquarium, and who's been tailing us, correct?" Sebastian said.

"Who said I couldn't follow a lead if it was right under my nose?" Huey narrowed his eyes at Lauren. "You think I haven't heard the mean things you say about me? Well, now Uncle Ray is going to see that *I* was the one to uncover one of the largest art thefts ever to hit Philadelphia."

"I'm sorry, I never should have said those things about you, Huey. It was wrong on my part, and I apologize." She took a tentative step forward.

"Don't come any closer," Huey barked.

"All right. I won't," she promised, noticing out of the corner of her eye that as Huey focused on her, Sebastian was slowly inching his way around the presser. "And it really is quite something the way you've tracked us down and all, but do you really think Ray is going to believe you're the one who found the art in the first place? I mean, Sebastian here is a professional investigator. Doesn't it make more sense that he was the one who uncovered the goods?" Sebastian had neared a front corner.

"I think Ray will believe his own flesh and blood over a reporter who lied about a story—yeah, I figured that out, too, you know—or some stranger who came waltzing in under false pretenses to the paper. For all I know, he isn't even a real investigator."

Sebastian leapt. The gun went off. Lauren screamed.

She stood frozen as the two men landed in a heap and struggled. She strained to see in the dark, the lighter having skidded off. Had Sebastian been hit? Would Huey, who had clearly lost it, turn the gun on her?

She had to act. Do something. Sebastian had a gun, didn't he? But he and Huey were rolling around. How could she possibly search for it? Stupid, stupid.

She turned her head, frantically looking around for a weapon of her own, anything. The tote bag on the floor. Lauren grabbed the heavy candlestick. She willed herself to move forward. She couldn't see who was who, only one body twisted atop the other.

That didn't stop her. Lauren raised the candlestick. And lowered the boom.

The body on top slumped, a dead weight. She stepped closer. If she had brained the wrong man, she was still in a position to take out the second.

She heard a grunt. Saw arms gradually shift the top body to the side. She hoisted the candlestick overhead. The man on the bottom instantly rolled to the side—facedown. There was no room for hesitation. She slammed the candlestick down, but it hit the floor, the force reverberating through her arms. She went to raise it again.

And then she heard a muffled voice.

"Darlin', I know we've had our differences, but trust me, violence doesn't solve anything."

Lauren slowly lowered the candlestick and let her shoulders sag. Relief washed through her. She laughed and hiccuped at the same time. "I can't believe it. I hit the right person, after all. I was so worried I'd hurt you." Her hands shaking, she needed all her energy to rest the candlestick on the presser. Then she turned to check on Sebastian.

And saw it. The lighter. In the fight, it must have slid across the floor near the clothes rack, where a pair of tuxedo pants were hanging. A small trail of flames licked the botton of the fabric.

"Sebastian, fire!" she screamed. "All the clothes, the plastic bags, the solvents in the shop—this could be a disaster." In the darkness, she rushed for the fire extinguisher that she remembered always hung on the wall by the stairs. She yanked it off the hinges and swirled around, lifting the hose at the same time.

But Sebastian was already there, stripping off his leather jacket. He batted at the flames, pulling the pants from the rack, and stomping on them until all that remained was a pair of singed trousers and his own ruined jacket. He dropped it and trudged toward Lauren. His face was bruised. His clothes blackened and disheveled. But a quick inspection told her the gunshot had missed his body.

Lauren let the fire extinguisher tumble to the floor. "Thank God," she sighed.

Sebastian touched her cheek. "I know what you mean. Never did I think dry cleaning could lead to such an adventure." He gulped for air. "I think it's time you called in all your buddies on the police force and got Huey hauled away."

Lauren closed her eyes and leaned her face into his hand. He rubbed her jaw. "Just think of the headlines this story is going to make."

His hand stilled.

Her smile faded. And painfully, oh so painfully, the light dawned.

Lauren lifted her face away and swallowed. "There isn't going to be a story, is there?"

Sebastian lowered his hand. "I'm sorry. You have to understand."

Lauren waved him off. "The hush-hush nature of the commission's work and all that. I should have figured it out earlier."

"If it's any consolation, I'll get in touch with Ray and explain that as the sole remaining relative of Harry Nord, I decided that I preferred to keep the story private after all. That you were the soul of professionalism, and I admired your work tremendously and that my decision had nothing to do with any lack of ability on your part."

"Well, that should make everything just hunky dory," Lauren said, not feeling the least bit like celebrating. So much for her big career break. At least now that the mystery had been solved, there was a possibility of salvaging things between Sebastian and...

She looked at his shuttered expression. Oh, brother, the other shoe had dropped without her even knowing it. "Let me guess. I suppose *now* you're going to tell me that there isn't any story as far as you and I are concerned, either?" She held her breath in anticipation, but only for a moment. She didn't need to add oxygen deprivation to her list of woes.

Instead, she held up a hand. "Listen, no problem. I'm a big girl. It's not like I'm going to cause a scene, have some major case of the vapors, or throw myself in front of the next SEPTA train. They never run on time anyway." She paused, rubbing the side of her head. Then she pulled her hand away, the light well and truly dawning. "Now that I think about it, I bet you were hoping to avoid any confrontation at all. Yes, that would be more your style. You probably planned to send your fond farewell via a phone call or an e-mail. No, I know, a tasteful note enclosed in a box of a dozen long-stemmed roses. Very classy. Hardly messy at all."

"I never said it was anything more than it was." At least he looked her in the face when he said it.

Lauren shook her shoulders wearily. "No, that's right, you never said anything of the sort." But *she* had so much more to say. So much more she wanted to confess. What was the point? He'd already made up his mind.

"I'm sorry." And he was. Sorry that he hadn't trusted her, but even more, that he didn't trust himself to be able to give her what she deserved. He touched her face again.

She pulled back. "Don't." She studied his expression, but he showed her nothing. Yielded nothing. "The funny thing is, I almost believe you really do feel bad."

She ran her hand through her hair in frustration. "I'll call the boys in blue, and then I'll notify my parents and make up something about there being a tiny, accidental fire. I just hope the true story—that never was and never will be—doesn't get back to them."

13

LAUREN HUNCHED OVER her desk at work. She didn't care that she'd come in late and missed a Monday morning story assignment meeting. She didn't even care that she hadn't brushed her hair.

Things were bad. Bad enough that she was listening to a CD on her Walkman and crying.

"Lauren, dear, the bed-head look is fine for punk rockers. Not so good for beat reporters."

Lauren lifted her head and wiped her eyes. "Phoebe, I think I've lost it." She slipped the earphones down around her neck.

Phoebe examined the CD case on Lauren's desk, next to her blotter. "No wonder you've lost it. You're listening to Engelbert Humperdinck. It's all Donna Drinkwater's doing, isn't it?"

Lauren sniffed. "No, it has nothing to do with Donna. It's my fault. I was a coward."

"Nonsense, never beat yourself up over a problem when you can blame somebody else, someone inherently odious—Baby Huey, for instance. Where is the boy wonder, anyway? Rumor has it Ray's been on the phone dealing with some high-priced lawyer regarding some mischief the little nephew has committed."

"When it comes to Huey, committed is right." Lauren shivered. "But I really can't talk about it. And truthfully, it's the furthest thing from my mind, especially after this." She thrust a crumpled envelope toward Phoebe. "Open it up. It just proves the injustice of the world," she sobbed into her desk.

Phoebe stepped forward, peeled open the envelope and slipped out a plastic bag. She peered at the contents. "What is this? Some new species of peyote? Now I know you've lost it."

Lauren looked up, her eyes swollen and red. "Of course it's not peyote—you know I don't do drugs, even those with a time-honored tradition among the Native Americans. No, it's worse than that. They're seeds, tomato seeds that my father collected from his own plants. He gave them to me to give to Sebastian, and now Sebastian's gone." She dropped her head on the desk with a *kerplunk*. "Because I was too much of a coward and let him get away."

"Frankly, dear, unless you turned the key in the ignition to his car and set it on cruise control, I think the man should take some responsibility for *his* decision to leave," Phoebe countered. "Besides, if you really need to send the seeds, there's always FedEx."

"I don't want to use FedEx."

"Then UPS next-day service is also very good, or so my assistant tells me. I personally don't like to get too close to men wearing brown shorts."

Lauren moaned. "This is not an issue for the fashion police, Phoebe. This is about love. And I let it get away without putting up a fight—even if the man is too stupid to admit that he's not a lone wolf, and that he walked away from the best thing that's ever happened to him."

Phoebe crossed her arms and tapped a manicured fingernail on the sleeve of her Michael Kors dress. "Well, if you want to talk about a man unburdening his heart, this morning I was copied on an e-mail that contained the most blatant outpouring of love I'd ever read."

"That's nice." Lauren really wasn't up to hearing about other people's good fortune.

Phoebe arched her neck toward Lauren. "You didn't happen to check your e-mail did you?"

Lauren sat up and sniffed. "No, I got in late and I haven't worked up the energy to even turn on the computer." She searched for her box of tissues, then remembered she'd given it to Huey last Friday. Oh, the injustice of it all, yet again.

"Well, maybe you should." Phoebe paused. "There's something from Sebastian."

Lauren waved her hand in the air. "Oh, you mean his letting Ray know that he doesn't want the paper pursuing the story on Harry Nord, his supposed grandfather, anymore—citing family privacy and all that." She groaned. "I suppose I should start polishing my resume now."

Phoebe reached over and impatiently pressed the Power button on Lauren's computer. "No, that's not what he wrote. And if you could tear yourself away from wallowing in misery and sappy lyrics, you would know."

"Oh, all right." Lauren set her teeth together, and

when the computer booted up, she typed in the password to access her e-mail. Her messages appeared.

"See, that one." Phoebe tapped the screen with her finger.

Lauren opened it up, skipped the address and subject heading, went right to the message:

Dear Ray—
Please excuse the use of e-mail instead of a personal meeting, but urgent business required me to leave Philadelphia immediately. As you will see from the attachment, which delineates the nature of my employment, I am an art theft investigator attached to an international commission. We work in close concert with Interpol and the FBI.

For some time, we had been tracking the disappearance of priceless works of art from a small hill town in northern Italy, and we had reason to believe that a resident of Philadelphia committed the crime. Upon the request of our organization and law enforcement officials, we asked Ms. Jeffries to publish the obituary on Harry Nord, knowing full well that the information actually pertained to a certain Bernard Lord, aka Benny Lord, who we believed perpetrated the thefts. A condition of this request was that Ms. Jeffries keep her actions secret, thus preventing the possibility of a leak into the investigation.

Ms. Jeffries was reluctant to abuse her position at the Sentinel in any way, let alone fabricate a story under the guise of a real obituary, but we convinced

her that she would be doing her country and the peo-
ple of Italy an enormous favor.

Due to Ms. Jeffries's superior investigative skills,
she was able to uncover the whereabouts of the stolen
items, most of which have already been returned to
their rightful owners. As for Mr. Lord, alias Benny
Lord, local law enforcement officials have subse-
quently confirmed that a previously unidentified
drowning victim was, in fact, the suspect. The real
Harry Nord, who did indeed recently pass away,
was never involved in the crime. Ms. Jeffries plans to
submit an accurate obituary on his behalf in the near
future.

Owing to Ms. Jeffries's outstanding contribution to
this investigation, the commission and law enforce-
ment bodies believe that the usual protocol of main-
taining silence should be abandoned, and that Ms.
Jeffries should be allowed to freely publish the details
of the incident. The Italian government has further in-
vited Ms. Jeffries to Italy to celebrate the return of
these national treasures to their rightful home.

With best regards,
Sebastian Alberti

Lauren was stunned. She placed her hand on her
cheek and felt it grow cold. Her mouth dropped
open, her throat tightened. She slowly swiveled her
head and gazed up at Phoebe.

"Here, I think you might want to use these."
Phoebe dangled the keys to her Jaguar. "And please,
drive carefully. Unlike you, it's all I've got."

Lauren stared, dumbfounded, for a second. Only a second. Then she pushed back her chair and stood up. Yanking open the drawer, she pulled out her bag. "Thanks, Phoebe." She took the car keys. "You're a true friend. And if Ray comes looking for me, tell him I'm, I don't know, that I'm checking out the best deal on flights to Italy, but that I'll be back as soon as possible to file the story."

She leaned over and kissed Phoebe smack on the lips. Of course, one of the guys from production happened to be walking by. Well, too bad. "I'm out of here," she announced.

The phone rang. She glanced at it. "I don't dare pick that up."

"Let me," Phoebe offered. "If it's Ray, I'll tell him you've already left." She lifted the receiver. "Hello. Oh, yes, Mrs. Jeffries, it's Phoebe Russell-Warren. Good to talk to you, too." Phoebe listened some more.

Lauren made a nixing gesture with her hands and moved to leave.

Phoebe caught her and held out the phone. "I think you'll want to hear this."

"DO YOU REALIZE I'VE been driving all over the map, looking for you? First Georgetown, and now the boonies of Pennsylvania," Lauren shouted. She stood with her hands on her hips and stared at a sight she never imagined beholding.

Sebastian Alberti—seated on the back of a tractor.

And wouldn't you know it, Mr. *Très Sophistiqué* Designer Chic looked positively yummy in ripped jeans and a faded Crimson Tide T-shirt.

Sebastian turned off the motor and squinted.

"How'd you find me? I purposely don't give the address of the farm out to anyone." He slipped down from his perch to stand next to her, then held up his hand. "Sorry, I forgot. You're an investigative reporter—a good investigative reporter."

"A great investigative reporter. And I'll show you just how great." She reached in her bag. "Here," she said with a grunt.

Sebastian's eyebrows jumped. "So that's why you've come? To give me the second candlestick?"

"Frankly, I'd rather brain you with the candlestick." Instead, she handed it over somewhat less than gracefully.

Sebastian stared at the ornate marble object. "Where was it?"

"It was at the dry cleaners, after all. In your skirmish with Huey, the gunshot nicked the side of the Suzie, you know, the mannequin-thingy. When my father went to open it up to do some repairs, he found the candlestick inside. Benny or somebody else must have used it to replace a support shaft on the inside that had broken on an earlier occasion."

"That's it then." Sebastian shook his head. "Everything is in order."

Lauren stepped closer. The top of her head was even with the cleft in his chin, a chin that she noticed was covered with stubble. Sebastian Alberti minus a close shave was truly a dangerous specimen— dangerous to the heart, that is.

She poked him in the chest. "No, everything is not in order. Me, for instance."

He looked skeptically at her finger. "Didn't you get the copy of my e-mail to Ray?"

She poked again. "Yes, I got your e-mail to Ray, but that's not what I'm on about."

"It's not?" He wrapped his hand around her finger. "Hey, be careful. You might not realize this, but I bruise easily."

"You know, that's your problem in a nutshell—you're afraid of bruising if you get too close to somebody." She would have poked again, but he still held on—potentially, a sign of progress. Potentially.

"Well, I've got news for you," she continued. "Like it or not, you *are* close to somebody—me. And I don't just mean standing here. I mean that you—you infuriating Italian Southerner—you made me fall in love with you."

He cocked his head in disbelief.

But Lauren also noticed that he suddenly clutched her hand more tightly. "Yes, you did," she went on. "And like it or not, you care for me, too—I know you do."

She waited for a response. And waited some more.

"This is where you're supposed to tell me that if you can just get over protecting yourself from getting hurt, you'll come to realize that maybe, just maybe, you could fall in love with me, as well," she ventured in a somewhat long-winded display of encouragement.

Still she waited. And waited some more.

Until finally Sebastian gave her hand one last squeeze before letting go. "I can't tell you that." He turned and carefully placed the candlestick on a wheel hub of the tractor.

Lauren clenched her jaw and glanced at the rich

soil at her feet. Slowly, she raised her head. "And I can't tell you how sorry I am to hear you say that." She moved to step away.

But he caught her by the hand and pulled her back. "I can't say that because I've already fallen in love with you, *bella*—with your strength, your intelligence, your wit, your beauty. And you're right—I was protecting myself. The thing of it is, I've been doing a lot of thinking about that."

He shook his head. "Guys and their mothers, right? I know it's a cliché, but in this case it really is true. You see, my mother didn't just walk out on my father and me, she walked into the arms of another man—the coach of the rival high school football team. It's silly I know, but at the time, to a lonely boy just beginning to fit in, it was the ultimate humiliation. And ever since, I made a point of not putting myself in a position to be betrayed—yet again. And the best way to do that was to cut myself off from caring for a woman, from wanting to get close." He breathed in deeply. "But with you, that was impossible."

Lauren swallowed. Hard. "So what are you saying? That we should work on seeing each other on weekends? See what grows from there?" She reached back into her bag again. "Which reminds me, my father gave me these tomato seeds from his garden for you to plant."

Sebastian pulled her close and circled his arms around her, resting his hands on the small of her back. "I'm saying that weekends aren't enough. Not for the tomatoes, not for us. Not nearly enough, not now and not in the future. Lauren—" he brought his lips close to hers and grinned mischievously "—I think we really need to follow the words of a wise man."

"What wise man?"

"You have to ask what wise man in matters of the heart?" he asked in mock horror. "Why, Engelbert Humperdinck."

"And what words by the maestro were you thinking of in particular?" Lauren asked, knowing already but wanting to hear them out loud, anyway.

"That I want the last waltz with you."

She beamed. "And like the song goes, 'The last waltz lasts forever.'"

And for now, their kiss did, too.

Epilogue

Six months later, the following appeared in the Lifestyle section of the *Philadelphia Sentinel*:

Lauren Jeffries
Sebastian Alberti

Lauren Jeffries, the daughter of Alice and George Jeffries of Philadelphia, was married yesterday to Sebastian Alberti, the son of Giovanni Alberti of Hunstville, Ala. and Isabella Reed of Athens, Ala. The Rev. Clyde O'Phelan officiated at the Hanover, Pennsylvania farm of the bridegroom.

The bride, 27, formerly Metropolitan reporter for the Philadelphia Sentinel, *is a staff reporter for the* Washington Post. *She is also under contract for a book on international organizations involved in locating stolen art. She graduated from Villanova. Her father owns Jeffries French Dry Cleaning in Philadelphia. Her mother works in the family business and is a wallpaper expert.*

The bridegroom, 31, is an art theft investigator for the World Organization for Retrieving Stolen Art. A magna cum laude graduate of University of Alabama, he served in the Marines in Desert Storm, and later obtained a master's degree in art history from Yale. His father is an engineer for the NASA research facility in Huntsville. His mother is a homemaker and president of the Garden Club of Athens, Ala.

After a honeymoon in Italy, the couple plans to reside in Washington, D.C., and Hanover.

The bride and bridegroom wish to assure friends and family that this announcement is the genuine article and not a hoax.

USA TODAY Bestselling Author

KRISTINE ROLOFSON

**welcomes you back to Texas—where the babies
are cute and the men are downright sexy!**

Enjoy

#989 THE BEST MAN IN TEXAS
(Sept 04)

#993 MADE IN TEXAS
(Oct 04)

*Available at your favorite bookstore
or online at eHarlequin.com*

www.eHarlequin.com

If you enjoyed what you just read,
then we've got an offer you can't resist!

Take 2 bestselling
love stories FREE!
Plus get a FREE surprise gift!

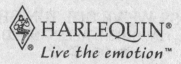